DEATH OF A TIN GOD

ALSO BY GEORGE BELLAIRS

Littlejohn on Leave
The Four Unfaithful Servants
Death of a Busybody
The Dead Shall be Raised
Death Stops the Frolic
The Murder of a Quack
He'd Rather be Dead
Calamity at Harwood
Death in the Night Watches
The Crime at Halfpenny Bridge
The Case of the Scared Rabbits
Death on the Last Train
The Case of the Seven Whistlers
The Case of the Famished Parson
Outrage on Gallows Hill
The Case of the Demented Spiv
Death Brings in the New Year
Dead March for Penelope Blow
Death in Dark Glasses
Crime in Lepers' Hollow
A Knife for Harry Dodd
Half-Mast for the Deemster
The Cursing Stones Murder
Death in Room Five
Death Treads Softly
Death Drops the Pilot
Death in High Provence
Death Sends for the Doctor
Corpse at the Carnival
Murder Makes Mistakes
Bones in the Wilderness
Toll the Bell for Murder
Corpses in Enderby
Death in the Fearful Night
Death in Despair
Death of a Tin God
The Body in the Dumb River
Death Before Breakfast
The Tormentors
Death in the Wasteland
Surfeit of Suspects
Death of a Shadow
Death Spins the Wheel
Intruder in the Dark
Strangers Among the Dead
Death in Desolation
Single Ticket to Death
Fatal Alibi
Murder Gone Mad
Tycoon's Deathbed
The Night They Killed Joss Varran
Pomeroy, Deceased
Murder Adrift
Devious Murder
Fear Round About
Close All Roads to Sospel
The Downhill Ride of Leeman
Popple An Old Man Dies

DEATH OF A TIN GOD
AN INSPECTOR LITTLEJOHN MYSTERY

GEORGE BELLAIRS

OPEN ROAD
INTEGRATED MEDIA
NEW YORK

All rights reserved, including without limitation the right to reproduce this book or any portion thereof in any form or by any means, whether electronic or mechanical, now known or hereinafter invented, without the express written permission of the publisher.

This is a work of fiction. Names, characters, places, events, and incidents either are the product of the author's imagination or are used fictitiously. Any resemblance to actual persons, living or dead, businesses, companies, events, or locales is entirely coincidental.

Copyright © 1961 by George Bellairs

ISBN: 978-1-5040-9250-0

This edition published in 2024 by Open Road Integrated Media, Inc.
180 Maiden Lane
New York, NY 10038
www.openroadmedia.com

DEATH OF A TIN GOD

1
LITTLE TIN GOD

Littlejohn wondered where he'd seen the man before.

He was tall, well-built, handsome, and dressed in an expensive suit of grey tweed. He moved in the aura of a V.I.P., which was confirmed by the way in which the stewardess of the Aer Lingus 'plane and a number of teenaged passengers were behaving. They hovered around him breathlessly and some of them asked for his autograph on any pieces of paper they could lay hands on.

Two days before, Littlejohn hadn't even thought of holidays, although it was the time of the year when business was comparatively slack at Scotland Yard. The crooks were migrating abroad or to fashionable English resorts, following the tide of holiday-makers. The July of a splendid English summer. Even in London, the air seemed spiced with the breath of the sea, and the sun was hot and bright and eager.

Then, Clara Tebbs had vanished. There was little news for the headlines at the time, and the dailies had given Clara a real fanfare.

LONDON SHOPKEEPER VANISHES

Miss Clara Tebbs, who keeps a corner shop in Shepherd's Bush, vanished into thin air yesterday in Dublin. One of a party of thirty-seven on a day trip, she left the coach from the air terminal in O'Connell Street and has not since been seen...

There followed a description and a photograph. The question on the lips of all who saw the portrait was: "Who'd want to run away with Clara Tebbs?" She was fifty-four, small, thin, and tired-looking through hard work. The dailies gave their readers the comfort of saying that the Dublin police and Scotland Yard were on the job. Through the absence of a colleague on holiday, Littlejohn had become involved, and when a message arrived from Dublin to say that the Irish police had found Clara, unconscious, in a city hospital, he'd decided he had better cross to Eire to identify her. When he arrived, it wasn't Clara at all. The woman in the hospital had been claimed already.

However, a consoling telegram had arrived at Dublin police headquarters.

See from news that you are in Dublin. Counting on you to call here for a day or two on your way home.

It was from the Rev. Caesar Kinrade, Archdeacon of Man, and his old friend.

So, here he was.

There was an atmosphere of suppressed excitement in the aircraft, as though something phenomenal was going to happen at any time. The V.I.P. was sitting alone in a seat in front of Littlejohn's. There was a scent of male cosmetics on the air. Littlejohn was trying to read, but from the looks of the hostess, he was sure he was committing a sacrilege or discourtesy. Finally, the girl could stand it no more. She bent smiling over the Superintendent.

"The man on the seat in front of you, sir, is Hal Vale."

Hal Vale! That was it! The film star. What a man to kick up a fuss about! Divorced three times and now ready for his fourth marriage. Darling of the hot press columnists and slick photographers.

"Who's Hal Vale?"

He couldn't help it!

The hostess gave him a compassionate look. Even Mr. Vale half turned and then decided he'd perhaps better not.

"Don't you know, sir? He's the famous film star. Crossing now to the Isle of Man for his sequences in a new film they're doing there."

The girl was in full spate.

"The film company's been there on location for over a week. He's joining them now. The film's called 'Women Who Wait'. He plays opposite the French star Monique Dol. You'll be coming across them, I'm sure, sir."

God forbid!

Hal Vale was snapping his fingers angrily for another drink. Some of the other occupants of the 'plane almost rose to get it for him, but the hostess was first.

Littlejohn was glad when they touched-down at Ronaldsway airport. The restlessness of the man in the seat in front bothered him. He was aware he was on parade and couldn't keep still for a minute in his almost vulgar efforts to attract attention. As soon as they drew-up on the tarmac, Hal Vale, who had been sulking to himself most of the journey, combed his hair, patted his tie, and assumed the smile-that-wouldn't-come-off. Like someone with his jaw and teeth struck immobile in the act of saying 'Cheese!'

There was a cheering crowd waiting for the 'plane at the airport, but Littlejohn had one small triumph. His friend, the Archdeacon, was the only person, except officials, allowed to meet him at the door of the 'plane itself. The rest were held back by regulations only a beloved Manxman could ignore. Hal Vale, emerging last from the aeroplane for effect, gazing momentarily at the two men greeting each other so warmly. One with a magnificent froth of white beard, bright blue eyes, shovel hat and gaitered legs. The other, massive, smiling, and genuinely glad to be there. A different kind of greeting from the one waiting for Mr. Vale from the huge crowd of fans and cinema actors and technicians. They were soon passing the star round from hand to hand, tearing at him, kissing him, and paying him the homage due to a little tin god.

Littlejohn and his friend detached themselves from the admiring mob and made for an ancient taxi, standing impudently among the magnificent vehicles brought by the film company.

The reception party gave another cheer as Hal Vale dutifully embraced Monique Dol, an elegant pretty little French blonde with shadowy eyes and a sumptuous half-naked bosom. The cameras flashed and the discreet scent of the masculine cosmetic, expensively advertised by Vale in person over television, mingled with Monique's perfume, made specially for her, and named *Damnation*.

The airport police-sergeant was excited, but not by the film-stars. He took up the telephone in his office.

"Give me Douglas police, Inspector Knell... That you, Inspector? Superintendent Littlejohn's just off the incoming 'plane from Dublin!"

Littlejohn's taxi was driven by a countryman, Teddy Looney, who looked like a character-actor from one of Marcel Pagnol's waterfront scripts. He was in trousers and shirt and wore a soiled light cap cocked over one eye.

"Good to be puttin' a sight on ye, Inspector."

Littlejohn had been promoted years ago, but the news hadn't yet reached Teddy!

And then a run through the exquisite Manx country into the interior, where the hidden village of Grenaby nestled by its clear stream, far away from the sophistication of the airport and its motley new arrivals.

Meanwhile, things were moving at Ronaldsway. The groups

were sorting themselves out in order of precedence. Hal Vale, Monique Dol, and the director, a man called Agostini, specially over from Rome to direct the Manx shots in true native fashion, headed the royal procession in a large expensive car, and the rest followed. It was all very gay. The airport was bathed in sunlight, so bright that it made people look like shadows in the glare. In front, huge beds of roses and flowering plants, and farther off, a long spit of rocky coast, an hotel, a ruined oratory, and then a strip of blue sea.

Finally, Ronaldsway settled down to its routine again, the staff glad to resume their usual jobs. The whole business had been banal and artificial, something of no importance, one which would soon be forgotten. Like those dull trivial bodily aches and pains, however, which suddenly flare-up and develop into a dangerous fatal malady. The next time Hal Vale arrived at the airport he was in his coffin.

The procession made its way swiftly to Douglas. Hal Vale took no interest in the scenery en route. He said he was tired and he looked it. There were bags under his eyes and his pouting mouth was drawn. Monique Dol caught his mood and sulked at his lack of attention, and Signor Agostini, certain in his mercurial mind that the pair weren't going to work well together, beat his fat knees in despair.

The flags were out in honour of the fresh arrivals, flapping from the two towers of the new luxury hotel, the *Carlton*, in the middle of the promenade. Next morning, they were to be brought down to half-mast. But more of that later...

A cocktail-party had been arranged at the *Carlton* to introduce the stars to the public. The room was packed with guests who were soon to be disappointed, for Hal Vale, after ten minutes of it, declared himself exhausted and retired for a rest to prepare himself for the dinner to be held that night. Monique Dol said she, too, was tired, and left with Vale.

At five o'clock, the bell rang in a small room on the first floor of the hotel where a maid and a waiter were quietly gossiping. A green light glowed over a label marked *Suite One*.

"It's Mr. Vale," said the maid, and hastily tidied her hair and gave her face a wipe-over with a powder puff.

The bell rang again.

"All right. All right..."

She hurried away and soon was back.

"He wants a valet. He's lying on the bed with his shoes and jacket off."

"What condition is he in?"

The waiter had served a bottle of whisky as Vale retired almost an hour earlier.

"The bottle's half empty on the bedside table. He mustn't be quite himself; he's squirted the soda all over the bed."

"Better get Sam. Where is he?"

They found the valet in his own room on the top floor, listening to the racing results over the radio. Without hurrying he made his way to Suite One where the signal lamp was still showing above the door.

Vale was lying on the bed, his collar and tie off, his hair tousled. His eyes were half-closed, his lips half-open, his hands crossed over his heart like a corpse. He turned on his side and opened one eye.

"It's taken you a hell of a time..."

Sam apologised.

"Next time I ring for you, see you come pronto. Now get out my evening clothes—tails—and you can shave me."

He sat up on the bed and thrust his fingers through his hair.

"Blast all this fuss! Why can't they leave me alone?"

The valet, who had unpacked for Vale, quietly and methodically got out the necessary clothes and other paraphernalia. Then he took an electric razor from a leather case and a bottle of shaving lotion.

"Shall I use the electric razor, sir?"

"What else? I never use any other."

Sam moved a chair under a light and stood erect to show he was ready. Vale settled himself and Sam shaved him. As he did so, he wondered what the women saw in him. Vale had a good figure and physique, true. But his face was petulant and hard. Anybody could see what a woman was in for with a man like him. And yet they kept coming and asking for more. Divorced three times, and now on the way to a fourth wedding, it was said. There was a rumour that Vale had been carrying-on with Monique Dol. It annoyed Sam. He liked Monique. A nice little dish, and kind and generous to all the servants.

"How much longer?"

"Just another moment, sir."

Vale was dark and tanned, probably with the help of a sunlamp. At close quarters his skin was coarse. It was said that he'd started at the bottom of the film world. A stand-in for somebody. He was still ill-bred and infantile under his veneer of sophistication.

Sam ran his fingers round Vale's cheeks and chin. A good shave. Smooth and tidy.

"Will you dress now, sir?"

"Of course not. It's not six yet. Draw me a bath and I'll soak for half-an-hour. Come back and help me dress at half-past six."

Sam drew the bathwater. Under cover of the splashing he expressed himself candidly and *sotto voce* about Mr. Vale. He stirred in bath-salts of the brand over which Mr. Vale purred on the television. When he returned to the bedroom, Vale was wearing a bathrobe and drinking another whisky and soda.

"That'll be all, then, till half-six. And be here. Don't let me have to ring for you."

"Very good, sir."

Sam gathered up and disposed of the clothes which Vale had flung about the place, and cleaned the razor.

"Don't put the shaver away. I might need to give myself another once-over later. Leave it on the dressing-table and go."

Vale lit a cigarette and made his way a bit unsteadily to his bath.

At exactly half-past six, the valet returned. He quietly let himself in No. One with his key and stood for a moment in the doorway. The lights were on and the bathroom door was open. All was silent. On the air, the scent of Vale's bath-salts. Sam could almost hear him saying, in his unctuous nauseating television voice, 'So, do as I do, and use *Maskuleen*, the virile cosmetics for fastidious men.'

As Sam walked the distance between the outer door and the bathroom, he half sensed that something was wrong. Vale had seemed to like all the lights on in the room, as though he were afraid of the dark. There were three in the bathroom and he knew they were all burning. As he passed the dressing-table he noticed the leather razor-case was lying there open. Surely Vale—damn him—hadn't had another shave!

The bath was behind the bathroom door and the first thing that Sam noticed was that over the washbowl a wire had been plugged in the electric-razor fitting. The other end of the wire was in the bath. He then saw the body of Hal Vale twisted and rigid in the tepid water. It appeared as if he'd scented danger, had half risen to avoid it, and death had taken him as he tried to get away.

Sam made an impulsive move to touch the body. Then, he realised what had happened and removed the plug over the washbowl. He knew from the nature of the white plastic-coated cable what was at the other end—the end lying in the bath under Vale's body. It was the electric razor.

The valet did not touch anything else. He hurried out to the bedside telephone.

"Hello! Give me the manager."

The manager thought it was Hal Vale and spoke in his most obliging voice.

"Hello, sir. What can I do for you?"

"It's me, sir. Sam, the valet..."

"Well? What is it?"

"Could you come to Suite One, sir. I've just found Mr. Vale dead in his bath."

There was a bronchial gasp at the other end.

"Don't touch a thing and don't tell a soul. Stay where you are till I get there."

The valet didn't know what to do whilst he waited. He measured the contents of the bedside whisky bottle with his eye and saw threequarters of the contents had been drunk. The syphon was on the floor and an ashtray had been overturned, as well, sprinkling a dozen or more cigarette ends and ash over the carpet.

Hurrying footsteps, and the manager appeared. He was breathless and excited. His hair was grey and his face was grey as well. He wore a black jacket and striped trousers and under the lights looked cadaverous. Outside, the Salvation Army band was passing in full blast. "Shall we gather at the river..." The manager rushed and closed the windows.

"He's in the bathroom. I think he's been electrocuted. You'll see."

The manager stood for a second, his knees knocking. Electrocuted! If it had been caused by faulty wiring in the hotel, someone was going to have to pay a pretty packet in damages. He peeped round the door of the bathroom.

"I wouldn't touch anything, sir. It's a job for the police."

"I know. I know. Ring for a doctor. Doctor Macleod. Tell him it's urgent..."

Dr. Macleod lived just behind the hotel and was there in less than five minutes.

"Suite One," said the receptionist who also operated the switchboard.

There was nothing for the doctor to do. Vale was quite dead.

"You've told the police?"

"Not yet..."

The manager looked completely stricken. Just his luck. An hotel full of guests and a unique occasion... a film company and two famous stars. And Vale had gone and electrocuted himself by trying to shave in his bath! It wasn't good enough!

The manager rang up the police station.

"An accident... Electricity? Hal Vale... The film star? Dear me! What a sensation... Yes... We'll be over right away."

The policeman at the other end of the 'phone was full of inappropriate jocularity!

The doctor had left things as they were, too. He stood by the dressing-table eyeing the room. It was a sumptuous one, specially laid-on for the famous guest. Everything tiptop, except that someone had missed dusting the cobwebs off the chandelier. His eyes fell on the razor case.

"He ought to have known better... Shaving in the bath with an electric razor. It's asking for it."

The valet had been standing by the bed, almost unobserved in the turmoil.

"What beats me, doctor, is that, half an hour before, I'd shaved him. His face was as smooth as a baby's... As smooth as glass. Why should he want to shave again?"

The manager glared at Sam. He wasn't paid to ask questions or show signs of unusual intelligence.

Sam told the same tale to the police when they arrived, and to the rest of the staff, and to the reporters who followed. To everybody, until they were sick of hearing it.

Meanwhile, in an identical suite on the floor above, Miss Dol's telephone was ringing. Nobody had given her a thought during the trouble in the rooms below. In another large hotel, the *Fort Anne*, a Mr. William J. Armstrong was trying to get Miss Dol.

"Please get me Miss Monique Dol at the *Carlton*."

"Certainly, sir."

Mr. Armstrong was a financier said to be interested in the new film, but he was fastidious, liked a quiet life, and preferred not to live with the publicity and vulgar advertising which went with the technical side of the business. He was very popular at his own hotel.

The telephonists at the *Carlton* and *Fort Anne* were friends, although they'd never met in person.

"Miss Dol, please, Betty."

"For Mr. Armstrong?"

"You might know..."

Silence on the line.

"She doesn't answer."

"Is she out?"

"Just a minute. I'll ask."

Another silence. The girl at *Fort Anne* could hear noises going on in the hall at the *Carlton*. There was even music playing. *Parlez-moi d'amour* on a trumpet.

"Hello, Jean. She's supposed to be in her room, but doesn't reply. I'm ringing now. What shall I do?"

"I'll ask Mr. Armstrong."

Another pause.

"He says she *must* be there. There's a party on. Publicity. She wouldn't miss that."

"You're telling me! I'll send up to her room and then ring you back."

The hall-porter said he was sure Miss Dol was in.

"Go up and see," he said to one of his lackeys, a youth in a brass-buttoned uniform, with a face and hair like a teddy-boy's.

The page-boy made for the lift.

"Walk up," said the hall-porter. "How many times...?"

When the boy eventually arrived at the door of Suite Two, he smoothed his oily hair, straightened his uniform and fingered his side whiskers, for he was a masher who'd taken a fancy to Monique Dol. Then he tapped on the door.

"Miss Dol..."

He did it three times and then shook the door handle.

A passing chambermaid called to him.

"What are you up to?"

"Miss Dol's wanted urgent and don't seem to be in."

"Well, what are you botherin' about, if she's not in?"

"The 'all-porter says she *is*."

"We'll soon see, then."

The girl opened the door with her pass-key.

"Here. You stop where you are. I'll go in. She might be in the bath."

The boy gave a wolf-whistle.

The maid was back.

"She's not here... I'd better speak to the hall-porter myself."

She sent the boy down again and returned to the bedside 'phone in Suite Two.

"Give me Mr. Peak, the hall-porter..."

"... Miss Dol's not in her room and I'm sure she's gone, and taken some of her things. The wardrobe door's open and there's clothes scattered about and a case missin'..."

"I'd better report to the manager. See you don't let this get out."

"As if I would."

The hall-porter, a massive figure who'd once been a blacksmith until trade grew bad, solemnly went to the manager's office to do his duty. He found him out and rang to Suite One.

"Excuse me, Mr. Kerr, but I've to report that Miss Dol's not in her room and it seems as if she's left the hotel. Packed a bag and gone somewhere..."

Mr. Kerr flung up his hands in dismay. He and the doctor were still waiting for the police. The doctor gave the manager a searching look and seemed uncertain whether or not to take his blood-pressure, auscultate his chest, or give him a hypodermic injection.

"Miss Dol's missing. It's thought she might have gone away somewhere..."

He ran from the room and up the next flight of stairs to make sure he wasn't dreaming it. The doctor followed him and they were joined by others on the way, all running as though the place were on fire. The room was still empty.

"I wonder if she's killed Vale and bolted," Mr. Kerr said to himself.

"But not with an electric shaver... What am I thinking of...?" He corrected himself reproachfully. His eyes fell on the small procession behind him. "What do you all want?" he said, and tried to make out that running from floor to floor was part of his usual routine.

The hotel was filling up. Tables had been booked by outsiders in the hope of joining in the evening's events. People were beginning to gather in the hall and bars. Others were sitting around expectantly in chairs, and at the reception-desk an obvious honeymoon couple were checking-in.

The manager rang up the police again.
"I think I ought to tell you that Miss Dol's disappeared. Miss Dol, D O L... The film actress... She's gone. Your men are on the way...? Oh, dear. I do hope they'll be discreet. The hotel's full. Any scandal might... Very well. I'll look out for them."

The manager gathered together the hall-porter, his acolyte, the room-maid and the valet.

"Now, all of you, not a word of this to anybody else. Understood? Otherwise, you're out."

Then he went outside and peered up and down the promenade hoping to spot and intercept the police. He looked like a modern version of the father on the look-out for the prodigal son. He even shaded his eyes dramatically with his hand, although the hotel porch was in shadow.

Finally, he saw the familiar car with *Police* over the roof. To his fevered imagination the letters were a yard high. He ran to meet it. Inside was sitting, with the chauffeur, a tall, well-built man with large teeth and a disarming smile.

"I'm so glad it's you, Inspector Knell. You're a reasonable man, I know. Could you drive up the side street and enter by the staff door? The place is full and the arrival of the police will cause a panic. Thanks."

On the way up the staff stairs, Mr. Kerr briefly told Knell what had happened. He was so immersed in his talk that he continued climbing after the first floor and he had to lead them down again. Like the famous Duke of York!

"As soon as it gets out, the press'll be here. Not only the Island press. These are international notables. I wish it had happened out of season. We've not a room to spare."

In Suite One the manager, the doctor, and the valet told Knell their stories.

"Accident, or maybe suicide?" said Knell.

"What I want to know is, why did he want another shave after I'd given him a perfect one only half an hour before?" asked Sam.

Knell rubbed his long chin.

"A funny way of committing suicide if he wanted to do away with himself."

His eye fell on the bedside table on which were spread bottles of throat lozenges, aspirins, indigestion tablets and phenobarbitone pills.

"If he'd made up his mind, he could have found a far better way..."

"Can we get him out of the bath now and away to... Well, I suppose it'll be the mortuary, won't it?"

"We'll see to that. It's a coroner's job. What about Miss Dol? Were they...?"

"It's rumoured that as soon as Mr. Vale's divorce is properly through, they're getting married."

The bedside telephone rang, just as Mr. Kerr was about to say that the *Carlton* was a respectable hotel and that he didn't cater for or allow carryings-on under his roof.

"It's for you, Inspector," said the manager, handing it over. It was from the police station.

"Yes, Knell here."

"The sergeant at the airport has been on, Inspector. He says he thinks he ought to report that Miss Dol, the film star, left the Island in the London 'plane. She seemed in a bit of a hurry and was lucky they'd a seat to spare..."

Film stars of international repute. Suicide or worse in a large hotel full of people Knell wasn't used to handling. The flight of Monique Dol, whose bosom was the toast of the day...

Knell's brain began to spin. Then, he smiled and took up the telephone again.

"Give me Castletown 5538... Grenaby parsonage. Ask for Superintendent Littlejohn."

2

EXIT HAL VALE

"You see, people in their class need careful handling. The limelight is always on them and half the world is interested in every little thing they do..."

Mr. Kerr thought he ought to give Knell a word of warning and advice. He was anxious that the reputation of his hotel should not suffer by the present tragedy. In fact, he hoped to get some good publicity from it if it were carefully handled.

A feeling that something was wrong somewhere was creeping like an ill wind round the *Carlton*. And, as Vale and Monique Dol had not shown up, suspicion was beginning to turn in their direction. The newshawks and photographers were prowling the corridors and finally one of them took a couple of flashes of Knell closing the door of the bedroom in the very face of Anatole Beanstock, producer of the film. Beanstock had almost forced his way in the bedroom; and Knell had almost thrown him out.

"You have to be careful..."

Mr. Kerr looked like a doleful spaniel begging for his tea.

Knell, who lived a quiet homely life with his family in a modest semi-detached house in the suburb of Onchan, felt respect, almost fear, in the face of all this luxury, this high-living, this artificial stage on which the characters were picked out in floodlights for the adulation and stimulation of millions of readers of newspapers, magazines, gossip columns and on radio and television.

"An ideal policeman should be all things to all men," he'd once read in a manual.

Knell was finding it a bit difficult. But he'd done quite a lot of good work before the public began to grow restive and intrude.

First, the hotel electrician. His name was Kinley and he was good at his job. A little dark man, with overalls a size too big for him. He looked about to slip out of them at any time and reveal himself clad in mere shorts and singlet.

"Oh, yes. The government regulations don't specific'ly prohibit the installing of electrical points for razors in bathrooms. We're all right there. If it was heating plugs, that 'ud be a different matter."

"How is it the lights didn't fuse when the razor was dropped in the bath?"

"These shaver-points are on a separate circuit, you see. Like as not, it would put off all the other razor-points on this floor. I can't understand why it didn't, but then perhaps nobody's tried 'em yet. The fuse-box is in a cupboard on each floor. If the fuse had blown, Mr. Vale might not have been killed."

"Why didn't the fuse blow?"

"I'll just go an' have a look at it."

Mr. Kinley left leisurely to investigate. He was soon back holding aloft a piece of tarnished wire.

"Somebody took out the ordinary thin fuse-wire and put this in instead. It's ordinary power-plug fuse-wire. A bit strong for a razor-plug, but nowadays these amateur electricians couldn't care less. They're always messin' about with things they don't understand. This wire looks to 'ave been in for some time. And the fuse-box hasn't been opened for donkey's years. It's full of dust."

The razor itself had been examined, too. It was Vale's own. An expensive model, evidently well-used.

"If it 'ad been a new one with the case watertight, there's less chance he might 'ave been killed."

"Make a note about all that," said Knell to the bobby at his elbow, who was thumbing a large shiny notebook.

The constable made an eager entry.

And, next, if it wasn't an accident or suicide, who had been able to enter the room whilst Vale was in his bath? Knell sent for the valet again. Sam had been excluded from the room as unnecessary. He returned with a smile of triumph.

"Yes, sir."

"You were the last in the room before Mr. Vale died?"

"I suppose so. I left the key on the table."

"Was Mr. Vale in his bath when you went?"

"No. He was messin' about in his bath-robe."

"Did you put away the electric shaver when you finished with it?"

"No. I cleaned it and left it in its case on the dressing-table, along with his brushes and manicure things."

"In the case?"

"Yes. Just so he could find it if he wanted to give his face a run-over later in the evenin'."

"Who else would have a key to this room?"

"The floor-maid... and there's one in the office. I have one, too. The manager will have a list. All, except the duplicate one in the office, are master-keys to fit all the rooms."

Mr. Kerr nodded.

"Would you like the list? Only the staff have them."

"I'll see it later. Who might be likely to want to get in the room? I don't mean a murderer. That we'll see to later. Anybody you know of?"

The manager coughed. He dreaded the idea of scandal in his hotel.

"All I can think of, is Miss Dol. She might have wanted to see him about something. The filming, perhaps. Or, on the other hand, he might have sent for her and let her in."

Knell picked up the bedside telephone.

"Were you on the switch, miss, when Mr. Vale and Miss Dol retired to their rooms late this afternoon? You were. Did he ring her or did she ring him?"

The answer came that Vale had rung Miss Dol.

"What did he say?"

She didn't know. She wasn't in the habit of listening-in.

Knell looked at the manager. He was eagerly waiting to know what happened.

"Excuse me a minute."

Knell hastily left them and ran downstairs to the main hall. The place was agog. Curiosity had infected the lot of them. When Knell appeared, there was a silence, as though they expected him to shout aloud and broadcast a bulletin.

"What's happened, Inspector? Give us a break."

He was surrounded by reporters. He brushed them aside.

"Is it true Vale's dead?"

"I'll see to a statement later. I've nothing to say just now."

The hall-porter led Knell to the telephone room. A dark, good-looking girl was sitting at the board, pulling out switches and putting them in again. She was busy. Everybody was ringing the hotel, asking for news, trying to book tables for the dinner later, wanting to confirm the rumour which had begun to circulate in the town.

"Can you find a substitute for Miss...?"

"Miss Macnab. Yes..."

The porter hurried out and came back with a blonde this time. The earphones were passed from the dark to the fair one. Miss Macnab eyed Knell suspiciously.

Knell dismissed the hall-porter.

"Now, Miss Macnab. Just a word in private with you. Did you

or did you not overhear a conversation between Mr. Vale and Miss Dol just after they'd retired to their rooms after the cocktail party?"

She was preparing to deny it again. Knell raised his hand.

"Listen, Miss Macnab. I want the truth. I know it's not done to listen-in to telephone conversations, but this one was most important. As you know, Mr. Vale is dead..."

The girl nodded; she wasn't surprised.

"I want to know who was last in his room. Did Vale ring Miss Dol and ask her to come to him? If you give me the truth, I'll see you don't suffer for it. But you can't tell me that one so interested in film-stars as you must be, given a chance to overhear a conversation between two such celebrities, would miss it. Now... What was said?"

"If you won't tell the manager, then. He just said 'I want to see you, Monique. Come to my room right away.' She said, 'I'm just getting in my bath...'"

The girl blushed.

"He said 'All the better. Come as you are.' She didn't reply to that. So he just answered, 'Come as soon as you can, then.' And he said he was going to have his bath, too, but he'd leave the door just ajar, so she could get in."

"Was that all?"

"Yes. He hung-up, then. He was angry about something, judging from his tone of voice."

"Any more calls to or from the pair of them?"

"No, sir. Mr. Armstrong tried to get Miss Dol several times. He's staying at *Fort Anne* and was a friend of hers. He often rang her up. It's said he financed the film they're doing here."

"He spoke to her?"

"He spoke to her this morning, but we couldn't get her for him when he rang this afternoon after she left the cocktail-party."

"Thank you."

"You'll not mention it to the manager that I...?"

Knell promised and ran the gauntlet of the hall again. A constable had arrived and was keeping guard at the door of Vale's suite. He saluted Knell smartly.

The curtains of the bedroom were still drawn, but someone had opened that of the little side window, a long narrow slit through which the late sunlight was shining. Mr. Kerr, the hotel manager, was standing near the bathroom door like a watchdog, and Sam, the valet, who seemed to be forgotten, was leaning against the dressing-table.

The body was still in the bath and all the lights of the bathroom were on.

The telephone rang at the bedside. The manager, who was nearest, took it up after a questioning glance at Knell.

"Yes? Who? He's coming up...?"

Everyone looked expectant.

"It's Mr. Armstrong. He's a director of the film company. It's said he provided most of the finance for this film."

Mr. Armstrong appeared. A man of about fifty, with silver hair, a small grey moustache, sunburned, and dark-complexioned. He was tall and powerfully built, and wore a suit of fine light-grey worsted. He looked round the room and his eyes fell on the manager.

"What's going-on here, Kerr?"

"I'm sorry, Mr. Armstrong, Mr. Vale is dead."

Armstrong's eyes opened wider and his eyebrows shot up.

"How did it happen?"

Mr. Kerr coughed.

"This is Inspector Knell, of the Douglas police. He's handling the case."

Armstrong turned to Knell.

"Well?"

Here was another of them! One who belonged to a world quite alien to Knell's. A sophisticated, level-headed wealthy man, who probably thought money would buy anything.

Knell pointed to the bathroom.

"He's been found dead in his bath. Please don't go in, sir. I may as well tell you, the cause of his death is under investigation. We found an electric razor in the bathwater and Mr. Vale had been electrocuted."

Armstrong nevertheless put his head round the bathroom door and stood for a minute looking at the body in the water.

"An accident?"

It was just at that moment that other footsteps were heard along the soft carpet of the corridor.

"Who's this?"

Knell's impatient tone suddenly changed and he hurried to greet the newcomer. A large, fresh-faced, urbane man, who almost filled the doorway.

"Hullo, sir! How are you? I *am* glad to see you..."

He turned to the rest.

"This is Superintendent Littlejohn, of Scotland Yard."

Introductions all round. It might have been the beginning of another cocktail-party instead of a murder investigation. Knell, in his delight, overdid it a bit.

Mr. Armstrong seemed really surprised this time.

"Have they already called in the London police?"

"I'm on holiday, sir. I heard Inspector Knell was here and came to see him. We're old friends."

Knell seemed to grow a couple of inches taller.

"I'd better tell you all about this matter, sir, but I must talk to you in private."

Knell gave the rest an eloquent glance.

The manager, professionally tactful, opened another door and indicated a room which nobody had entered hitherto. A small, elegant drawing-room, the curtains of which were pulled back, revealing the magnificent sweep of Douglas Bay. Littlejohn followed Knell, who screwed up his eyes at the bright light after the dimness of the bedroom.

He briefly told Littlejohn what it was all about, explaining step by step what he had done since he arrived and what he had found out so far. Then they returned to the bedroom. The rest were still there.

The manager made for them eagerly.

"Do you need me any more? There are matters to attend to. There's a dinner, too, arranged by the film company in honour of Mr. Vale. I don't know what we'll do about it."

He glanced at Armstrong.

"It'll be cancelled, of course. See to it, Kerr. And get some of those busybodies out of the hotel. The place is overrun with them."

"We'll have to make a statement for the newspapers. We can't get away from that. Shall I say there's been an accident?"

"Until the police are certain about the cause of death, you'd better."

He turned to Littlejohn, whom he now obviously regarded as in charge.

"That's right, isn't it?"

"Yes."

The manager turned to go and then was back again.

"What about Miss Dol? What do we say about her?"

Armstrong looked rattled.

"She isn't dead, as well, is she? Where is she?"

"She's gone. Inspector Knell had better tell you, sir."

Knell seemed to have forgotten Miss Dol.

"She's left by 'plane for London. We've asked the police there to keep us informed after they've enquired at the airport. We've not heard anything further yet."

Armstrong was flabbergasted.

"This is serious. The film can't go on with the two main stars out of it. I'd better get along and see what's happening and make some arrangements."

Littlejohn emerged from the bathroom.

"Before you go, sir, I'd like a brief word with you."

"Won't it do later?"

"I'm afraid not. Let's go to the drawing-room again."

Armstrong turned to Sam.

"Go and get me a bottle of whisky, a syphon, and some glasses. It's time we had a drink. We need it after all this."

Almost right away a small boy in a white coat arrived with the drinks. He was followed by the manager, who looked more put-out than ever.

"Excuse me, gentlemen, but more police have arrived, and the coroner's men. They're drawing-up in a car at the front. Would it be in order for me to conduct them through the staff entrance? You understand, Superintendent. The main hall is full... And if..."

"Ask Inspector Knell. He's in charge."

"And may I also ask... if... if the body is conveyed to the mortuary, it may also be removed by the side door?"

"Ask Inspector Knell..."

The manager withdrew backwards, like someone leaving royalty.

"Whisky, Littlejohn?"

Armstrong was pouring out a helping in a glass.

"Not just at present, sir."

"Very well."

He helped himself and filled up with soda.

Armstrong sat in one of the armchairs and crossed his legs.

"I suppose you're aware that Hal Vale is a very important man?"

"Is he, sir?"

"Of course he is, and you know it. No use being awkward about it. He's top of the tree in the film world and in newspaper headlines every day. The same applies to Miss Dol."

"How old was Vale?"

A pause, as though his age didn't matter.

"Around forty. He's right at the top and the full limelight's on him."

"He lives in London?"

"Yes."

It was said irritably, as though that didn't matter either.

"Where did he come from originally?"

"I don't really know. London, I think. He was a workman in a studio and some director or other noticed him. He was a stand-in, they tell me. And then he got a small part. After that, he didn't stop till he was right at the top."

Armstrong kept rubbing it in, as though, somehow, in spite of the fact that he was dead, he wished Vale to receive special treatment.

"Was he a great friend of yours?"

"Yes. We met on the Riviera about five years ago. I financed a couple of films for him. I'm what might vulgarly be called his backer."

"You're not staying at this hotel?"

"No. I want peace and quiet. All this publicity and ballyhoo bores me. I like to keep my distance."

"You were also a friend of Miss Dol?"

"Yes. One meets these people in the film world. We've been friends for a year or two."

"What were Miss Dol's relations with Mr. Vale?"

Armstrong remained perfectly calm.

"What have you been hearing?"

"That they've been about a lot together of late."

"I gather what you mean. That is true."

"Vale has been married three times?"

"Yes."

"The third divorce is about to become absolute, I understand."

"That is true. Within the next few days."

"Was Vale on good terms with all three women?"

Armstrong took another drink and gave a shrug. Then he pulled a cigarette from a gold case and offered one to Littlejohn.

"Smoke?"

"No, thanks, sir."

"These marriages and divorces aren't taken very seriously, as you probably know, in the film world. It's a fantastic, hothouse atmosphere of which those who don't inhabit it have no idea."

"Did Vale pay alimony to all of them?"

"Officially, yes. But two of them are wealthy enough to manage quite comfortably without it."

"So, his death might not greatly upset them?"

Armstrong raised his eyebrows, like someone shocked.

"You're not suggesting...?"

"I'm suggesting nothing, sir. Had Vale any enemies?"

"I don't know of any."

"As regards Miss Dol... Could it be that she had reasons for wishing Vale out of the way?"

"Certainly not."

Littlejohn looked Armstrong straight in the eyes.

"When the third divorce became absolute, did he and Miss Dol intend to marry?"

"Yes, I think they did. Vale I know, wished it."

"And she?"

"Yes. She's also been recently divorced and has many men friends. I think, however, Vale was her favourite."

Littlejohn smiled. He could imagine Monique Dol having a list and making her choice. Every day she seemed to be about in public with someone fresh.

"You were in the habit of seeing Miss Dol frequently, sir. Was that a matter of business?"

Armstrong emptied his glass and then poured himself another drink.

"What do you mean by that, Littlejohn?"

"It was owing to the fact that you tried to ring her after she returned from meeting Vale at the airport, that it was discovered that she'd left the hotel and taken a 'plane to London. You must have been eager to speak with her."

Armstrong shrugged.

"I merely wished to ask her if Vale had arrived safely and if the reception—it was a cocktail-party—had gone off all right. I didn't attend myself. As I said, I hate publicity. Will there be anything more?"

"I think not, for the present. Do you intend staying on the Island for long?"

"I can't tell you, yet. If Monique returns quickly, we may go on with the filming. You see, Vale was detained on another contract and hadn't made an appearance in the film. It was a matter of filling-in. Now he will have to be replaced. Miss Dol, however, has been on location for almost a week and if she doesn't finish, it may mean scrapping the lot. So, you understand, I must wait and see."

"In any event, you'll let us know where we can find you. You know so much of the background of this affair that we are sure to need your help later."

"I'll keep you informed. But surely, you can't wish to detain all the company indefinitely. They can't be kept more or less in exile here till the case is solved. That is, *if* it turns out to be murder..."

"It looks very much like murder, sir. Vale had already had a good shave when he entered his bath. Why should he want another? And Miss Dol has vanished into the bargain. I don't suppose the company will be breaking-up and leaving for a day or two. We'll consider the rest later."

"May I go, then?"

"Yes. Have you any idea where Miss Dol might have gone?"

Armstrong hesitated.

"Not, as yet. She might have gone anywhere."

"What did she do before she took to films?"

"She's been on the stage ever since she left school. It's in the blood. Her father was a prompter at the Comédie Française."

A prompter! That was a good start indeed!

There was a knock on the door. It was Knell and with him, the police surgeon, his bag in his hand. Armstrong bade them good-bye and brushed past them.

"Quite a big shot in his way," said the doctor. He was a long, lean emaciated man, with sad baggy eyes and a large moustache.

"Is it Vale?"

"Yes."

"I was playing golf and they brought me away on the sixteenth hole."

He sounded disappointed about something.

Littlejohn and Knell took him in the bedroom and Knell pointed to the bathroom. The photographers and other technicians were gathering up their implements and packing them away. All the curtains were now drawn back, revealing to the full the expensive furniture and fittings. Odds and ends belonging to Vale were scattered about. His personal effects were all costly. A travelling-clock by Cartier, a heavy gold cigarette-case, a silver manicure-set.

Vale's trunks must also have arrived in advance by sea. The wardrobes were full. About eight suits and a dozen pairs of shoes.

Dr. Finlay, the police surgeon, sounded to be talking to himself in the bathroom.

"Drunk when he got in the bath, by the looks of it. All the signs of death by electric shock. We'll have to make a post-mortem and I'll let you have the full report after it..."

Littlejohn opened the drawers of the dressing-table and chests. All neat and tidy as Sam had left them. In the top drawer of the dressing-table, a letter case, in fine leather with a Bond Street name. It was crammed with papers of all shapes and sizes. Letters, bills, invitations, tickets, and many from women, mainly fans, mixed with business notes.

Littlejohn handed it to Knell.

"Better take that with you, old chap, and run through the contents when you've time. What about Miss Dol's room; has it been looked over?"

"Yes, sir. Like to see it?"

They didn't wait for the lift. The room was almost a replica of Vale's own below. Only there were feminine touches about it. Mr. Kerr had used a lighter hand. The furnishing was dainty, the fittings brighter. The scent of *Damnation* hung over it all.

Miss Dol must have left in a hurry. Her wardrobes, too, were choc-a-bloc with clothes. Dresses of all kinds galore; over twenty pairs of shoes. An opened bottle of champagne and a half-full glass on the little table near the bed.

More letters, bills, invitations, fan mail in two of the drawers. Knell collected the lot, although there didn't appear much among them of any importance.

The room maid, who was summoned, said the wardrobe had been open when she entered and found Miss Dol missing. There was still an open B.E.A. timetable on the bed, which was littered with clothes as well, as though Monique Dol had hurriedly sorted out a few urgent requirements to take with her on her flight. Her jewel-case had, the maid said, also gone.

In the bathroom, the bath was filled with scented, soapy water and *Damnation* bath-salts! A bath-robe crumpled on the floor, towels scattered about. Everything indicative of haste.

Outside, the detectives met a dismal procession coming from Vale's room. A stretcher borne by two men, and on it, a covered form. The doctor had finished with Vale for the time being and now the body was on its way to the morgue. Mr. Kerr was leading the way, almost walking on his tiptoes, anguish written over his features, for he wished to get it all over before any of his clients appeared. The men with the stretcher wobbled heavily here and there in their efforts to avoid furniture and the expensively decorated walls.

Solemnly the cortège made for the back staircase, vanished through a door at the end of the corridor, and they could hear them bumping down the uncarpeted back stairs, marking time as they negotiated the narrow steps and acute bends. Finally, the body of Hal Vale, the brief and most recent showpiece of the *Carlton*, was carried through the luggage exit and deposited in the medico-legal tumbril.

In Vale's room, the telephone rang and Knell hastened to answer it. He took the message with surprise and at once passed it on to Littlejohn.

"Miss Dol seems to have given London the slip. She arrived a bit before we telephoned them, and the Manx 'plane was in and the passengers dispersed before the police got there. They searched the records to see if she'd taken a 'plane elsewhere. She had. A private one. She's gone to Nice."

Knell looked completely bewildered. Film stars, murders, international complications...

"What next, sir? The French police?"

Littlejohn rubbed his chin.

"We don't know how far Miss Dol is connected with the death of Vale, although, somehow, she seems mixed-up in it. But she's a film-star, remember, and therefore ranks almost with royalty. Can you imagine what will happen if she's quite innocent of the whole business and we ask the French police to detain her? I think I'd better go to Nice myself, unofficially. I can try to contact her, question her, if she'll co-operate, and then return in a matter of a couple of days..."

"I could fix it all with the Chief Constable, sir, if you'd be so good."

Be so good! Littlejohn never refused an opportunity of seeing the Mediterranean again!

No sooner said than done. The Manx police would be glad of his co-operation. He could fly out to London by charter 'plane that evening and get the first flight to the Riviera in the morning.

Littlejohn wondered what his host, the Archdeacon, would have to say. The Rev. Caesar Kinrade was quite excited about it over the telephone.

"I'll come with you!" he said.

Littlejohn took up the phone again. Whitehall 1212. Scotland Yard.

"Ring up the Sûreté at Nice, please. Get hold of Inspector Dorange. Tell him I'm flying out by the first 'plane from London in the morning. And ask him if he can find out if and where Monique Dol, the film star, is staying on the Riviera..."

And that was that. What a holiday!

3
ANOTHER WORLD

Whilst Littlejohn was telephoning—still from the bedside instrument at the *Carlton*—Knell, searching through the papers found in the dressing-table drawers of Monique Dol's room, came across a large packet addressed to her at Rue du Chevalier de la Barre, Paris. It looked like an old catalogue envelope, was postmarked Paris, 1957, and was filled with snapshots of all kinds.

"Have you seen these, sir?"

Littlejohn turned the pile of photographs over. They were all higgledy-piggledy, like a mass of playing-cards after a game. Knell did his best to shuffle them into something like order.

They must have been taken by a score or more of different cameras and collected all over the world. Some obviously on the Riviera, some in Paris, others in America. The kind of things one amasses from temporary friends on flying visits.

Monique Dol appeared on most of them, clad in almost every type of dress, from evening gowns to bikinis and, on one, she was naked. On the back of this was scribbled "Heliopolis". Many of her companions were well-known film personalities.

"Had Miss Dol a maid with her?"

Mr. Kerr, the manager, was back, standing in the shadows, like a forlorn spirit. The scene of the crime seemed to fascinate him. It was as if he expected the police to unearth some sinister secret which would completely ruin his hotel and himself and he could not bear to leave them alone.

"Miss Dol had a maid when she arrived. A girl called Clara, who didn't understand English. She had a row with Miss Dol and left. After that, we provided a maid from the hotel staff."

"Had she a business manager or an advertising agent with her?"

"Yes. Augustin Meunier. Everybody calls him Gus. He's below, shouting the place down because the police won't let him come up."

"Will you send for him?"

Mr. Kerr went for Gus himself; on the trot. He seemed happiest when scuttering violently about.

Augustin Meunier was a small, dark, hatchet-faced man, with close-cropped hair and one of those swarthy faces which make their owners look to need shaving four times or more a day. Gus was in a fury. He spoke English with a Franco-American accent.

"What's going on here? How is it I can't speak with Monique? Where is she?"

He flung his arms about.

"Miss Dol has left the Island. She has gone to Nice."

"She what!"

"You heard, Mr. Meunier. I haven't time to answer a lot of questions. I'm going to ask *you* some before I go to France to find her..."

"Who are you?"

Littlejohn told him.

"From what I hear, Vale's dead. She had nothing to do with it. Monique isn't that sort."

"I've not time to discuss that either, Mr. Meunier. I want you to answer my questions. You can ask as many as you like of my colleagues when I've gone. Why should Miss Dol flee to Nice?"

"She's gone to see Paul. Who else?"

"Who's Paul?"

"Her second husband."

"She was married three times?"

"Yes. Why?"

"You're her advertising man, I understand, Mr. Meunier. You must be a mine of information. Who were her three husbands, all divorced?"

"That's easy..."

Gus slipped an indigestion lozenge in his mouth. He looked as if he needed one. His complexion was grey and the skin hung in folds on his cheeks, although he couldn't have been much above forty. Every now and then, he nervously swallowed air.

"... First husband was Count Carlo Santamaria. An Italian. She married him before she got on the films. He was a waster. She ditched him when she met Paul. She married Paul. He was much older than her..."

"How old is she now?"

"Twenty-seven..."

"And Paul?"

"Fifty-eight. Look here. Mind if I have a drink?"

Meunier's face twitched. He lived on his nerves.

Mr. Kerr—still there—rushed out clapping his hands for attention. He was anxious to keep the film pundits in a good temper.

"Whisky and soda, I want. That's the only drink my doctor allows me. I've got ulcers."

"And the other husband?"

"John G. Malcolm, the film magnate. They met in Hollywood. *He* ditched *her*. The divorce hasn't been through long."

"Tell me about Paul. Why has she rushed off to him?"

"For advice, of course. She always goes to Paul."

"In spite of the divorce?"

"Sure. They're still good friends. She calls him uncle."

Mr. Kerr, who was back and listening-in, shrugged his shoulders and spread out his hands in wonder and despair.

"Who is Uncle Paul? What's his real name?"

"Paul Mauron. He's Swiss. He's a banker. Owns ironworks in Switzerland, too, a car factory in Luxembourg, silk mills in Lyon, and God knows what else elsewhere."

"Does he live in Nice?"

"He's a villa in Cannes, a house on Lake Geneva, a château in Provence, a flat in Aix-en-Provence..."

"Right. That will do for now."

"But he mostly stays in hotels. Monique and Paul have always been good friends. He's like a father to her..."

"Uncle, you mean?"

"Let's say both."

For the first time, Gus smiled. Then he swallowed air again as though the effort had been too much for him, and lit a cheroot. He was scared of cigarettes.

"What about John G. Malcolm?"

"He fell for her when she was doing a picture for him. He's a bit older than Monique. Quite a bit. He ditched her because of Hal Vale."

"I see. Not quite so broad-minded as Paul?"

"Paul's a man of the world. They got bored with being married, Monique and Paul, so agreed to break it up. They've got along fine since. Far better than when they were married."

"And you think she's flown to him?"

"If she's in trouble, that's where you'll find her."

Mr. Meunier rolled his cheroot dismally round his mouth, bit lumps from the end of it, and spat them about nervously.

"Can you tell me who's who among this lot...?"

Littlejohn spread the photographs about the table.

Many of them didn't need identifying at all. Actors, writers, faces which were always appearing in society papers, gossip columns, advertisements for cosmetics, patent medicines, jewellery and even dentifrice. Monique Dol's acquaintances were wide and varied. Gus shuffled the snapshots with a heavy forefinger.

"That's Paul..."

Littlejohn expected it! The harbour at Cannes; a luxury yacht; a tall, thin, aquiline man with a monocle in one eye, leaning over the rail nonchalantly. He was properly and impeccably dressed. On one side Monique Dol in a bikini, and on the other, a well-known opera singer looking unpleasant.

"This is John D. Malcolm..."

A little fat man with a hooked nose and a bald head, smoking a cigar in front of what might have been a country club. He looked very pleased with himself. Presumably taken before Hal Vale turned up. There was a photograph of a rajah, too.

"That's the ex-king of Berengaria and that one's Mr. Nim Nam Nung, the Burmese oil millionaire."

Gus himself appeared in another, looking ready to take an unwilling header into a sumptuous bathing-pool.

"Me!" said Gus, and threw his cheroot through the open window. It must have hit someone below, for a hoarse voice began to shout vulgar abuse.

"Thanks, Mr. Meunier. I think that will be all."

He took two pep pills from a phial, swallowed them with a drink of whisky, and looked even worse than before.

"All! It ain't all by a long way. If you see Monique, bring her back with you. Arrest her, chloroform her, handcuff her, but bring her back. She's under contract and unless she's right here by Monday—thank God tomorrow's Sunday—she's likely to be knocked for a hell of a packet. Tell her that. Although I guess Paul will pay up, as usual, if she runs out of lolly..."

Gus battled bravely in his American French and Littlejohn had to guess half of it and deduce a lot more of what he said.

Knell stood by, bewildered. This was a new world to him. The

Count, Paul, Malcolm, Gus... They were types he'd never encountered in the course of his duties on the happy Isle of Man.

In the lift on the way out, they met a famous English comedian, also in the cast, waiting to ascend. He looked anything but humorous. He was wondering if the whole business was ever going to finish. He seemed to have drunk too much and there were heavy bags under his eyes.

The hall was full of celebrities, too. This time they were not preening and exhibiting themselves. They eyed Littlejohn imploringly, eager for him to put an end to the suspense. Gus was still at Littlejohn's elbow.

"Don't forget to give Monique my message. Most of these people are depending on her. Tell her that."

Littlejohn glanced at them all. They certainly looked it!

"Had Mr. Vale a representative here?"

"Joe McLeary. He's gone over to England for the day. Attending to some contracts. Due back tomorrow. When he finds out what has happened, it'll kill him."

"Is he a lawyer?"

"No. Hal's lawyer's in London. A fellow called Firmin. He'll be over soon as the news breaks on the other side."

"Did he do all Vale's business?"

"I don't know. Monique mentioned Firmin to me once or twice. That's all."

There didn't seem to be a proper spokesman for the film company there. Anatole Beanstock had got himself drunk in despair, and nobody knew where Agostini had got to. Perhaps he'd thrown himself in the sea. Armstrong had gone back to his hotel where, presumably, he was telephoning to the mainland, consulting co-directors, lawyers and agencies about the future of the film.

"Let's go, Knell."

It was a warm dusk and people were strolling along the vast promenade enjoying it. The holiday season had started and the town was full of visitors. It all looked very pleasant. Horse-trams clopping along the asphalt, happy crowds milling about, singing popular hits, the sea in front, blue, placid, with the tide out, and behind, the gentle hills of Man, sweeping smoothly down to the waterfront.

And Hal Vale was dead and Monique Dol had run away to her 'uncle' in Nice.

Littlejohn would have liked to spend a lot of time lounging about, rubbing shoulders with the mixed crowd at the *Carlton*, questioning the hotel staff.

He would have to leave Knell to do all that. He and his friend, the Archdeacon of Man, were off to lay the voluptuous Monique, the talk of the town, by the heels, somewhere in the south of France. Littlejohn felt he knew her well already. The photographs, the contents of her rooms at the *Carlton*, her very aura about them, the ubiquitous scent of *Damnation*...

The Rev. Caesar Kinrade was waiting at the airport for Littlejohn. He was like a boy going on holiday. His eyes shone and he was eager and excited. They planned to dine in London when they got there.

Littlejohn made final suggestions about the case to Knell, who wrung his hand as though they were parting for ever.

"*Au revoir*, sir. *Bon voyage*..."

Knell uttered what was left of his schoolboy French and looked self-conscious.

"Good-bye, old chap. I'll keep in touch with you by 'phone from France..."

They were in London before eleven and stayed the night in the Littlejohn's Hampstead flat, where, in the absence of his wife, Littlejohn made some omelettes for supper.

At London airport next morning, they found a squad of journalists waiting for them. Someone must have passed on the news from the Island. Cameras flashed.

"What's the bishop going for?"

A reporter indicated the Archdeacon's gaiters and gave the old man a deferential salute. There was no answer, so, for the benefit of his readers, he made one up.

> HAL VALE IS MURDERED IN HIS BATH
> Scotland Yard called in.
>
> This morning, following a lead, Superintendent Littlejohn left for Nice. He was accompanied by Dr. Kinrade, Bishop of Man, and a well-known amateur detective. Good luck, bishop!

Littlejohn visited the office of the airport police, and checked that Monique Dol had left for Nice by charter 'plane. The English police had kept in touch with the French. Miss Dol, it seemed, had been picked up at Nice airport by a Rolls Royce which had then left in the direction of Cannes. There was also a message from the Nice Sûreté. Inspector Dorange would meet Littlejohn's 'plane.

They fought their way through the crowds to the passport and departure offices. Loudspeakers were blaring. Mr. Manoulescu was wanted by the Bagdad Airways and Mr. Mulcrone was asked to report at the Aer Lingus desk.

In the 'plane the hostess gave them a pleasant little speech of welcome, glucose sweets, then coffee. The Archdeacon was placidly reading. Some of the film characters he had recently encountered on the Island had reminded him of a favourite author he had neglected too long. He was reading Damon Runyon. Littlejohn was glancing through the daily paper but his thoughts were elsewhere.

He was glad of the Archdeacon's company. That invulnerable old man gave him immense moral support. Like Knell, Littlejohn was a bit out of his element in the present case. He had often before dealt with millionaires, business magnates, county families, playboys, débutantes. But now he was in another world. Film stars and their financiers didn't trouble him at all. But men like

Armstrong and Mauron were rare birds in his experience. Remote figures who stood apart from the rest, drawing vast profits, but aloof, frequenting the haunts of their kind in London, America, the Riviera, the international yacht clubs, the luxury hotels all over the world. They owned luxury homes, but rarely lived in them; they patronised and entertained politicians, film-stars, petty or passé royalty. Bankers, financiers, and cabinet ministers eagerly served their interests and, when they died, the event shook the world's stock exchanges although their names were not even mentioned.

Monique Dol had obviously made her way into this closed circle and was now en route to one of its members for help. If she had, in fact, murdered Vale, the police were up against a problem. Paul Mauron could pull strings, issue big cheques on most of the capitals of Europe, call on his friends or lackeys to go the limit to help...

And Hal Vale... Married three times, and, if it hadn't been for murder, he, too, might have entered the orbit of the Maurons, Armstrongs, Malcolms, by marrying Monique.

Littlejohn took out his notebook. Vale's wives.

The first had been Muriel Gibbon, an usherette in a London cinema. That had been the time when Vale was a scene-shifter and stand-in at film studios. He'd quickly outgrown her and married Irene, the wealthy wife of an author, Alan Botophe, whose books were filmed and who had divorced Irene because of Vale. Then, Marie de Beer, actress wife of a diplomat, who'd divorced her husband. When he died, Hal Vale had been waiting for absolute release from Marie and then it looked as if he'd marry Monique Dol. What a motley crew! Every marriage of Vale's had been childless and occasionally spectacular. Justin de Beer, for example, had given Vale a good hiding in a night club before they could separate them, and then gone to remote South America on duty. The usherette had remarried—an Italian, with vast refrigeration and ice-cream interests in Milan. Alan and Irene Botolphe were, it was said, together again.

Littlejohn looked out of the window and down on the vast, desolate wilderness of the Basses-Alpes, which on terra firma he knew so well, but which from the present height was quite foreign to him. The Archdeacon was asleep and on the seat across the gangway a man was reading *Mary Queen of Scots and the Babington Plot*.

They struck the Mediterranean west of Cannes and the 'plane slowly lost height over the blue water on the way to Nice. Yachts on the sea; a luxury liner approaching Antibes; fishing boats far out; the familiar coastline with bays, capes, rocks and islands spread out like a relief-map.

The hostess was saying her farewell piece.

Ladies and gentlemen...

Mesdames, messieurs...

The red light was on... Seat belts and no smoking. The 'plane touched-down. A guard of honour of policemen in white gloves was awaiting the 'plane and with them a little, keen-faced, smiling man with a red carnation in his buttonhole. He wore an almost white suit and snakeskin shoes and belt, and fell upon and embraced Littlejohn as soon as he set foot on the tarmac. Introductions. The Archdeacon and the little man exchanged warm handclasps and the Archdeacon addressed him in flawless French. He had, in his younger days, acted as chaplain in English churches in France, and still maintained an interest in them.

"I've heard a lot about you, Inspector Dorange."

In the restaurant of the airport an Englishman, dining with French friends at a table adjacent to the great windows, was explaining.

"It's the Archbishop of York, and the big man will be his private detective. He's over for an international religious conference..."

The crowds on the verandahs took snapshots and waved their

handkerchiefs at the Venerable Archdeacon, who stole all the limelight from a politician arriving on the same 'plane to discuss tariff reductions.

As usual, Dorange refused to talk business until they'd dined. They passed through customs and passports without any formalities. The balcony with the full view of the runways, and then, the sea, blue and still, with a tycoon's graceful yacht moving slowly in the distance to Monte Carlo.

"*Trois Pernods... Trois...*"

Dorange raised an eyebrow and smiled at the Venerable Caesar Kinrade, who nodded back.

They relaxed and sipped their drinks, watching the busy traffic of the airport. All around them flowed the stream of Riviera holidays, wealth, sophistication, stretched out in a long forty-mile line of corniche between Mentone and St. Raphael. Littlejohn remembered that, according to schedule, he should have been taking a rest at Grenaby. He looked at his watch. Noon. It would be absolutely quiet in Grenaby now. Morning service taken by the Archdeacon's deputy would just be over and the small congregation would be on its way home to Sunday dinner... Behind him, a waiter staggered in with a cargo of hors d'oeuvres and arranged them on a table. Then he brought whole lobsters, cold chickens and a ham, and spread them temptingly to attract his clients. At Grenaby, they needed no tempting, no appetising!

"You will stay with me whilst you're here," Dorange was saying. Which meant at the villa surrounded by rose and carnation fields, near Vence, where Dorange's parents ran a flower farm.

"Meanwhile, Monique Dol has stayed the night at Mauron's villa at Super-Cannes. He is there himself, but, for some reason, at ten this morning, Monique left in his car and drove in the direction of Aix-en-Provence. The road police have orders to report the progress of the car and I've no doubt that, in a little while, we shall hear that she has arrived at Mauron's flat in Aix, which seems to be her favourite retreat when she comes here. Enquiries at Cannes show that Mauron leaves there tomorrow for a trip to Greece in his yacht. He must have advised Monique not to travel with him, which, in view of the events in the Isle of Man, is good advice indeed."

Outside and at the bars of the airport, pilots and personnel from 'planes of all nations were chatting and drinking. An ambulance drew up at a charter 'plane and an invalid, looking more dead than alive, was gently transferred from one to the other.

A member of the airport police, clad in a light khaki suit, crossed hastily to Dorange and spoke to him, saluted, and left.

"Excuse me. A telephone call from Cannes."

Dorange rose and followed his subordinate. He was back in five minutes.

"A message from Paul Mauron himself. He has been informed of your arrival at Nice airport and would like to see you. The police also gave me the reason for Monique's early departure for Aix. It appears that another woman has arrived at the Cannes villa. It might be unwise for her to find Monique there already!"

Strange how Mauron and his types all over the world never missed a trick. Everywhere their representatives were scattered, seeking information likely to interest them, transmitting it to the centre of affairs, following events round the earth.

"We'll have lunch first, then. Mauron says he will be free at three o'clock at his villa. He asks us not to contact Monique until he has spoken to you. She is staying for the present at his flat in the Cours Mirabeau, at Aix, and he assures us she will remain there until you are satisfied that she had nothing to do with Hal Vale's death."

"He is very well informed."

"His kind always are. Better perhaps, than the police."

The holiday feeling, which always seized Littlejohn on such visits, was upon him again. And, judging from his expression, the Rev. Caesar Kinrade was feeling the same. His bright blue eyes were taking everything in from the small child of five, being conducted by a hostess to the Air France *Caravelle* for Paris and being handed over to another hostess to travel alone, to the man in handcuffs being hustled by a detective to the 'plane for Corsica. Then, he stood and frantically waved his hand to a man in a dark suit on his way across the tarmac to a B.E.A. flight for London. The man waved back enthusiastically.

"That's Finlo Collister, from Fildraw," he said. "There are Manxmen all over the world, wherever you go!"

Caviare arrived and one of the lobsters from the adjoining table; it looked large enough to feed a multitude. The waiter asked them how they would like their steaks cooking...

On the next table some people were asking for *bouillabaisse*, and in one corner, a beautifully turned-out woman of uncertain age was lifting a small poodle and placing it on the table, where it began eagerly to eat the food on her plate.

Then, the door opened again and a tall, powerful man in a lightweight grey suit and panama entered. He wore sun-glasses and carried a leather brief-case. He was obviously well-known and respected there, for the manager ran to greet him and the waiter convulsively danced attendance round him.

In spite of the sun-glasses Littlejohn at once recognised him and nodded to him. The man ignored him as though he'd never seen him before.

"The man in the corner, there, Dorange. Do you know him?"

"Certainly. He has a villa at Juan-les-Pins, and two vineyards near Draguignan..."

It was W. J. Armstrong.

4

MONTJOUVAIN

Armstrong steadily sipped his drink, yawned, and took off his sunglasses. It was like a badly acted melodrama. He rose, slowly walked to the table, and towered over Littlejohn.

"In case you wonder why I'm here, I'm not following you. I'm too busy for such things. No; I have a house here and I'm just moving in for a rest."

Then he turned on his heel and went out.

Nobody else had spoken and neither Littlejohn nor his friends seemed disposed to discuss the matter. Instead, Dorange beckoned a man who looked like a tripper taking an odd drink or two and watching mournfully the passersby. He, unlike his colleagues, wore a black suit in keeping with his melancholy face, and greeted the three of them deferentially.

"Keep an eye on the man who's just left," said Dorange. The man nodded without moving a muscle of his sad features and quietly went on his way. Whatever he later reported must have been lost in the files, for it never figured in the case.

That was as far as it went for the time being.

Dorange drove the little police-car to Cannes. It was a madcap race and here and there, where police on duty recognised him, they held up the traffic to let him pass.

Mauron's villa was high on La Californie and Dorange's driving was like that of someone on the dodgems at the fair as he tore up the road, which snaked its way by eccentric curves and gradients all the way to the Observatory at the top. Finally, they pulled up at a huge pair of wrought-iron gates. *Montjouvain*. A gardener urged them on and they continued along a path to the door of the villa.

A magnificent square building with a huge pepperpot tower at each corner, a coat of arms carved in the stone over the great front door, and exquisite gardens with English lawns undulating on every side and kept green by revolving sprays. A dovecote from which the birds kept launching themselves for short flights. From the terrace, a breath-taking view of the sea and coast from the Esterel to Cap d'Antibes.

Littlejohn slowly descended from the car. The holiday feeling was in his bones. He'd almost forgotten what he was there for. The penetrating sun and the blue sea always took him that way. The Archdeacon, in his black suit and gaiters, looked like a visitor from a strange land and made a dark shadow in the shimmering sunshine. Dorange rang the bell and a servant wearing a striped, sleeved waistcoat appeared and bade them enter. He didn't even ask their names.

"Monsieur is expecting you."

The hall was vast and square, with a high roof under which open first- and second-floor landings were visible with their artistic wrought-iron railings. The floor was of marble and a huge white marble staircase, with a passenger lift alongside, rose from the left. A fine great tapestry covered one wall. The servant led them to a door in one corner, opened it, and stood aside to allow them to pass. As they entered, a woman leaned over the balcony above and after looking down on them vanished into one of the bedrooms. She was almost naked, with her exposed skin amber from the sun, and was smoking a cigarette. She was fair and had a sad drooping mouth and large languid eyes.

The room was like one of a private suite in a luxury hotel. A salon-set of gilt Louis XVI chairs, a beautifully carved marble-topped table, exquisite mirrors on the walls, a rich carpet on the floor and, in one corner, as if keeping watch on it all, an imposing cast-iron head of a Chinese nobleman. From the roof hung a magnificent lustre chandelier. The shutters of the room were closed against the dazzling afternoon sunlight, but at an angle through them, a large swimming-pool was visible. The water was still and there was nobody there, except the gardener, surreptitiously kissing the maid, who made feeble protests.

Paul Mauron followed them in.

"Welcome, gentlemen," he said in English, shook hands, and addressed them each by name. He seemed informed about everything beforehand.

"Sit down."

And then, for the benefit of Dorange, with whose lack of English he also seemed acquainted, he switched to French.

"I believe that you, Venerable Archdeacon, and Superintendent Littlejohn, speak very good French."

His natural manner was surprising. He came and went from one to another of them, perfectly at his ease, as if he'd known them all his life, talking as if to himself all the time. He wore a light grey suit of woollen cloth so fine that it looked like linen, and a white silk shirt and a dark blue tie. He was easily recognisable from the snapshots which Monique Dol had left behind. Tall, slim, graceful, easy-moving and strong for all his sixty years. He was bald at the front and his head was bronzed from the sun.

The manservant entered with drinks on a trolley and served them with silent speed. As he did so, Paul Mauron talked with the Archdeacon about the Isle of Man. He had visited the Island once when his yacht put into Douglas Bay for two days to shelter from a summer storm. He had, it seemed, made the most of this time to explore the place.

Then Mauron got down to business.

"I know that you have traced Monique to Nice. She telephoned late yesterday afternoon to say she must see me. I arranged a charter 'plane from London right away. She hurried here to ask my advice as soon as she could after she found Vale dead in his bath. I told her not to run away, but to await your arrival at my flat in Aix, of which she's very fond. My car is at your disposal if you wish to make the journey to see her. You have not met her?"

"No."

"She is a very dear creature, but a mere child under her veneer of sophistication. Have you had any further news about the affair, may I ask?"

"No, sir. We haven't contacted the Island since we left yesterday."

"The news is out in the newspapers, I suppose."

"Yes. It was in the headlines when we left London airport. The reports weren't quite accurate, I'm afraid, but the death of Hal Vale and the flight of Miss Dol are now known."

"As regards Monique... One could hardly call it flight. She came to me for advice."

"Did she tell you how Vale's death occurred, sir?"

"She found him dead in his bath."

"Murdered would be more precise. I assume she didn't touch the body. Otherwise, she might have received a shock."

"She said not. She said his expression was so hideous that she fled back to her room right away, gathered a few things, and came here.

"Why would she do that if she merely thought he'd died naturally?"

"She said she had a premonition of foul play. She was badly scared and is very temperamental. It is quite like her to do as she has done."

"You've had details of what happened, sir?"

"Yes. I telephoned a friend of mine on the Isle of Man. He was interested in the film..."

"W. J. Armstrong?"

For the first time Mauron looked a bit surprised. Here was something, at last, that he hadn't foreseen.

"Yes. How did you know?"

"We saw him at the airport at Nice. He didn't seem pleased to find us there."

"Armstrong and I are business associates. He has interests over here, too."

"So he said."

"He told me how Vale had died. Electrocuted in his bath by an electric razor. Might Vale not have been shaving and let the razor slip?"

"No, sir. The valet had just shaved him. Did you know Vale well?"

"Well enough. I've business dealings with him. Film finance. He was also a friend of Monique."

Littlejohn was beginning to understand why Monique Dol, scared by the death of Vale, had fled to Mauron. Why she called him uncle, and in spite of the divorce, remained his friend. Mauron was reliable, powerful, and efficient. She could depend on him.

The servant was back filling up the glasses.

"You intend to go to Aix to see Monique?"

"Yes."

"You will understand when you see her, why she couldn't possibly have killed Vale. She's quite herself again now. Yesterday, when she telephoned me from London airport, she was completely incoherent and confused. She had apparently fled as soon as she found Vale. Packed a few essentials and hurried away on the next 'plane. She'd no money after she'd paid for her ticket from the Isle of Man to London. She persuaded one of the banks in the airport to cash a cheque for her. One of the clerks there recognised her. He'd seen her in a film..."

"She was your wife once, sir?"

It sounded queer said like that, but such things seemed mere commonplaces in this rarefied world.

Mauron nodded affably.

"For four years. We're still very good friends. She was doing small parts in films when we met. We married. Then, she went off to Hollywood. We were too long apart. She married Malcolm, who made several contracts with her for films..."

He was still smiling. If the idea of Monique's opportunist career struck him, he didn't show it.

He passed round his cigarette-case.

"One thing I wish to emphasise, Littlejohn. Monique's flight and strange behaviour must not be taken as evidence of her guilt in the Vale affair. She has always been that way. As soon as trouble appears, she runs away from it. As often as not, she runs to me. If you concentrate on her side of the case, you will make a big mistake and probably miss the real murderer..."

"Have you any idea who he might be?"

Mauron shrugged.

"Not the slightest. I've no idea of motive, either. Vale had been married three times. But his matrimonial adventures would provide no motive, I'm sure."

"Didn't the former husband of his last wife attack him once?"

"De Beer, you mean? Yes. But de Beer died last year in Nicaragua from fever and whisky."

"I believe that when his third wife's divorce became absolute, Vale and Miss Dol planned to marry. Is that so?"

"Yes. Are you thinking that perhaps one of her former husbands might have decided to kill Vale? Count Carlo, or Malcolm, or myself. Please cross us from your list. Carlo married again. The daughter of an Italian scooter millionaire..."

As might be expected! There seemed more than enough

tycoons with daughters to spare to console the free men of this rare world of divorce, mansions in the south, private yachts, and international finance.

"As for myself, our present arrangements suit me admirably and Vale could not possibly have disturbed them. In fact, I'm sure they would have delighted him. As for J. G. Malcolm... His brief spell as Monique's husband almost killed him. After a massive coronary occlusion which almost finished him, he couldn't get rid of her fast enough!"

"Yet all of you loved her at one time or another!"

Mauron raised his eyebrows.

"My dear Littlejohn! You are surely not trying to make the murder into a crime of passion! Men shooting each other or tearing at one another's throats because of Monique! Try to understand. Monique may be a pretty woman, amusing, passionate, especially on the films, but since she left Carlo she has been civilised, trained to live in a certain way, in a certain set..."

Mauron was suggesting that since he'd undertaken her education and introduced her to his circle and standards of behaviour, such vulgarities as murder through jealousy, lust, or revenge were unthinkable!

Dorange, who had opened the shutters of one window and was standing with his back to the room admiring the view, smiled and shrugged. He knew more of the varied levels and codes of society than most people. He also knew that Mauron himself would never stain his hands by killing an enemy. He would either encompass his ruin in other ways or else, by a telephone call or even a nod of the head, cause his quick extinction by someone else.

"Did Miss Dol tell you exactly what happened when she found Vale dead in his bath, sir?"

"Yes. When Vale arrived on the Island, there was a cocktail party in his honour at his hotel. He and Monique drank rather a lot and retired early to their rooms to rest ready for a dinner in the evening. Vale telephoned to Monique from his room. She was in her bath. He said he hadn't had a chance of a word alone with her and asked her to join him in his suite where drinks had been served. She said she would come as soon as she could. He replied that he would leave his door ajar as he was also going to his bath. That was the last she heard of him alive."

"And when she did go to his room...?"

"He was in his bath. She called to him, got no reply, and put her head round the half-open door of the bathroom. He was in the water and so obviously dead, so hideously dead, to use her own words, that she fled. There was nobody in the room, all the lights were on, and she saw nobody on her way there or on her return to her own suite. She was terrified and thought that if she'd been seen entering Vale's room, she might fall under suspicion and have a very bad time with the police. She fled to London, telephoned me from the airport, and I told her to come to see me at once. That is all I know. Maybe, she will tell you more when you question her at Aix."

Somewhere in another room the telephone was ringing.

"Excuse me. The telephone. My secretary is down in Cannes and the rest of the staff are in other parts of the house..."

Mauron hurried away. The man with the trolley of drinks appeared almost right away and sadly gave them fresh glasses of Martini. After he'd left, dead silence fell on the whole place. The Archdeacon seemed to be brooding on all the queer things he'd been hearing and Dorange was interested in what was going on in the garden.

Mauron apologised again.

"My skipper in Cannes. The yacht is ready. We're going on a trip to Greece tomorrow, early. We will sleep aboard tonight. I don't suppose it would be agreeable to you for Monique to go with us. She would, at least, be free from pestering by newspaper men if she were at sea with me."

"I think she'd better remain where we can find her, sir.

Besides, I was told to give her a message from the film company on location when I met her. Work has ceased and the film will be ruined unless she gets back quickly and takes her place again."

Dorange was smiling to himself. He knew that Paul Mauron had already made up his mind that Monique had better not join the sailing party. The half-dressed sunburned blonde upstairs was probably the reason.

"I'd better telephone her and tell her you'll be at Aix... tomorrow, shall we say?"

"Yes. Probably around noon. We'll go by road."

"Shall I arrange for the car?"

"No, thank you, sir. Inspector Dorange will be taking us in a police vehicle."

"Will you please remember then, Littlejohn, it would be a great favour to me if you'd treat Monique very kindly? I know you will. It's rather an absurd affair, isn't it?"

"I don't find it as absurd as all that, sir. I'm glad the rest of Vale's friends and colleagues didn't decide to scatter themselves all over Europe following Miss Dol's example. It was very stupid of her to do it. And it's caused the police a lot of trouble."

"I appreciate that, Superintendent. But Monique's that way, you see."

There was another pause in the conversation. Even Mauron seemed short of something else to say.

"It's all very annoying," he said finally.

"Certainly, sir. It is. It must have been more annoying, too, for Vale to be electrocuted in his bath, just as he'd got right to the top. You're sure you've no suggestions to make which might help us?"

"No. But I'll let you know if anything strikes me. We've telephonic contact from the yacht with the land..."

Of course they had! With irons in the fire all over the world and reports coming in from north, south, east, and west, Mauron would need to keep in touch.

"Have you arranged your hotel, Littlejohn? If not, I'll fix you up as my guests at an hotel here."

"Thank you, sir, but we're staying with Inspector Dorange..."

"Ah, at Vence."

He knew that, too! One wondered what Mauron didn't know!

He saw them off at the front door. Dorange had preceded them and they found him holding a shabby little man by the scruff of his neck. In the man's hands were all the paraphernalia of press photography.

"Just a flash, Inspector. Only one. Be a sport!"

"*Fiche-moi le camp!* If you take a single flash, I'll smash the whole bag of tricks. *Filez! Hop!!*"

"The newspapers are hot on the trail," said Dorange when he'd gone. "Very soon the whole nation will be in mourning for Hal Vale."

At Cannes police station, Littlejohn put through a call to the Isle of Man.

"Douglas police? Is Inspector Knell there? Littlejohn here..."

A joyful voice at the other end.

"Is that you, sir...?"

Knell seemed surprised at the clarity of the line.

"Where are you?"

"Cannes."

"You might be speaking from over the way in Douglas."

"Anynews...?"

Plenty. The press had got hold of the story and the place was full of reporters. Mr. Firmin, Vale's lawyer, had turned up, too, and played merry hell because he hadn't been advised of his client's murder, but had found it out casually. Someone had actually told him in a night-club when he was dancing with a lady-friend. It didn't look right and decent, dancing with Vale dead. Mr. Firmin had been made to feel a fool...

"I suppose you know Hal Vale's been murdered." Just like that, in the middle of a rumba!

W. J. Armstrong had vanished, too. He'd chartered a 'plane around the time Littlejohn had left, and gone off in it.

"He's here, old man. I've spoken with him. Or rather, he did the talking. He seemed annoyed to see me."

"In Cannes?"

"Nice. He has houses and vineyards here. We'll keep an eye on him."

"That's a relief! What about Miss Dol, sir? Have you seen her?"

"We're going to find her tomorrow. We know where she is."

"Good. The film company's still here. There's nothing else to report. We've questioned everybody. No good..."

The afternoon was stifling and Littlejohn felt he'd had enough. He rang off after telling Knell to do his best, and then he and Archdeacon and Dorange sat for half an hour in a café facing the harbour. It was apéritif time... *l'heure de l'apéritif*—and it was unusually quiet. Here and there sailors repairing gear or cleaning the decks and fittings of craft tied up in the harbour. They identified Mauron's boat. A magnificent motor yacht, all spick and span and ready for off. He'd even called it *Monique*! There were some of the party already on board, drinking cocktails under an awning. Young people wearing very little, and among them, rather out of date in a yachting-cap and blazer, an elderly man with silver hair and a grey moustache. He was a deposed Balkan king who'd been shot at three times in the street.

Nearby, a man in a sailor cap tried to persuade Littlejohn and party to make a trip in his motor-cruiser to the Isles in the bay. When he saw Dorange, however, he offered to take them for nothing.

A North African loaded with carpets, scarves and knick-knacks approached them with a broad smile, until he spotted Dorange. Then he beat it hell-for-leather.

They returned with Dorange to Vence, through Grasse and Pont-du-Loup. Dusk was falling and a soft light was beginning to silhouette the mountains against the clear sky. Here and there they passed through a hill-village, where all the inhabitants seemed to have turned out to take the air before night and stood festooned along the road, watching curiously all the passing traffic and trying to make out the occupants of the cars.

Vence was quiet after a busy Sunday. There was a sound of splashing fountains on the air. The locals were enjoying the warm evening, sitting at tables of cafés under the trees of the main square. Many of them waved at Dorange, whose car they recognised. Two miles away from Vence, on the Nice side, stood Dorange's home, a squat white house, built in colonial style, with a walled garden. All around were fields of roses and carnations which scented the warm air.

At the door they were met by Dorange's parents. A tall, elderly man with a small beard and a fine profile, whom the Archdeacon later said resembled his old friend R. B. Cunninghame-Graham. He wore a broad-brimmed hat like a sombrero, and was standing to greet them with an old lady, dark and still beautiful, like a Spanish aristocrat. They gave the visitors a warm welcome and for the rest of the night Vale and his death and his strange circle of friends were forgotten.

5
AIX-EN-PROVENCE

Littlejohn and Dorange left for Aix early the following morning. The Archdeacon stayed behind with his host, who had taken a fancy to him and insisted on his having a rest after the preceding strenuous day. Mr. Kinrade didn't need much persuading.

There was a faint mist over the rose and carnation fields, the haze of heat which precedes a sizzling day. As the party breakfasted, the air was filled with the fragrance of flowers and Littlejohn was sorry he wasn't able to stay there instead of chasing about the Riviera in search of a film star who had run away from trouble.

Monique Dol had found Hal Vale dead in his bath. She'd seen the body. Instead of informing the police right away, she'd taken the first 'plane and vanished. The poor girl! That was what Paul Mauron had called her. Poor girl, whose nerves were so bad, whose temperament so precious, that she must be forgiven for not behaving like others. Take the first 'plane to Nice and come to see me. Take refuge in the flat in Aix where you are always comfortable. I'll look after things. Mauron was sure he'd be able to see her through.

When Littlejohn and Dorange reached Aix, they found things weren't quite as easy as Mauron had expected. The press were waiting for them at the door. In the morning paper they'd picked up at Grasse, there was a front-page photograph. Mauron's affairs were always headline news.

A flash of Littlejohn and the Archdeacon getting off the 'plane. Dorange shaking hands.

> Superintendent Littlejohn, de Scotland Yard, arrive à Nice.

They took the shortest route to Aix, through Grasse and Cannes and then over the Esterel by the road passing Mont Vinaigre, and on to Fréjus. The heat was intense and open windows and the speed of the car gave little relief. Viewed from Cannes, the sea was like a quiet lake, with pedal-craft and small boats buzzing about at all the resorts. In the distance, they could make out Mauron's yacht heading for the east and Greece.

They crossed the Massif des Maures by the long dreary road to Brignolles, through St. Maximin, and then into Aix.

It was mid-day in Aix-en-Provence and, before going about their business, Littlejohn and Dorange lunched under the trees in the Cours Mirabeau. It was cool there and the splash of the many fountains in the avenue was refreshing. They ate *loup grillé et flambé à l'armagnac*, and *agneau des Baux arlésienne*, washed down with a cool *Château de Selle*. It was all very pleasant, the trees marched four abreast along the Cours and, at the summit, the statue of the good Roy René looked down benevolently on his beloved Aix, the finest little capital in Europe. The two detectives, instead of being able to sleep it all off, had now to seek out Monique Dol, the runaway film star.

Mauron's flat was on the Cours Mirabeau, too. The large town house of his ancient family stood back among the trees, too big for modern use, converted into luxurious flats, mainly with an eye to preserving the fine building by habitation than making it revenue yielding. Mauron had enough money without that!

On the news-stand at the bottom of the boulevard the late editions were displayed.

Hal Vale, film-star anglais, tué dans sa baignoire.
    Scotland Yard cherche Monique Dol.

And an awful photograph of Vale, looking like a wanted man. The kind you see on passports.

At the door of the flat, cameras flashed and newsmen accosted Dorange and Littlejohn and asked them for the latest.

"We know that Monique's inside, but we can't get at her. Is she suspected?"

A uniformed porter met them in the hall. M. Mauron had already telephoned. They were to receive every help and hospitality.

This place, too, was like a de luxe hotel. It was as though Mauron and his set could not bear any change in their environment and insisted on taking it with them everywhere they went. The decoration was like that at *Montjouvain*. A little more fresh and modern, perhaps, but fundamentally the same. Extravagant striped wallpapers, gilded exquisitely upholstered armchairs, expensive console tables, thick carpets on the floors, a fine gilt chandelier hanging from the ornamental ceiling.

"Is Miss Dol in?"

"Yes, sir; she's expecting you. I'll take you to the flat."

It was on the first floor, giving a fine view of the Cours Mirabeau, yet away from the noise and bustle of the pavements.

The porter let them in with his key, after knocking, and someone had called "*Entrez*". The flat was up to the Mauron standard. Antique furniture, rich, light wallpaper, a genuine Fragonard on one wall and, on the opposite one, a striking portrait of Mauron in the full regalia of some Order or other.

There was nobody in the salon, but sounds of someone moving beyond an open door at the far end. On the table in the middle of the room, a tray with a half-eaten meal... cold chicken, salad, rolls, one of them crumbled. And a bottle of wine and a used glass.

The porter gave them seats and left them.

"I'm so sorry I wasn't ready for you..."

Monique Dol had made her entrance.

Littlejohn had met the small, pretty woman standing before them many times, though not in the flesh. Her pictures were plastered all over the fronts of cinemas everywhere and the week-end journals and newspapers made regular features of her. *Autographed portrait of Monique Dol with every copy.*

Her négligé was familiar, too. Fluffy and diaphanous, with half her breasts showing. But now she was pale, only half made-up, worn and tired-eyed. Littlejohn wondered if this, too, were part of the make-up, assumed to give her an easy passage with the police.

Dorange certainly was unmoved. She shook hands with Littlejohn. The tired expression even extended to her grip. Dorange kissed the tips of her fingers, but in his gesture there was a trace of mockery, as though he were merely doing what was expected of him.

"Please sit down."

The room was filled with the faint scent of the famous *Damnation*. She sat opposite them in an armchair, her feet respectably together as becomes a good woman being questioned by the law. She wore white mules with gold filigree and the edge of her silk nightgown was visible below her peignoir. She'd obviously only just got up.

"I am sorry to cause you so much trouble. I ought not to have run away like that. He said it was very foolish..."

"You mean M. Paul Mauron?"

She nodded.

"Your best plan, then, is to return to the Isle of Man at once, Miss Dol. First, because the police there wish to ask you some questions. Secondly, you have your film contract to fulfil. The whole company's waiting for you."

She shrugged. She looked tired out and years older. And Littlejohn was sure she wasn't acting now, either.

"Paul told me the same. I will return later in the day. I'll leave Aix almost at once. Are you annoyed with me?"

She pouted as she said it and gave Littlejohn a sultry smile. He smiled back. After all, he owed to her this trip to a land he loved, but her infantile flight was exasperating all the same.

"No. But I'd like to ask you a few questions before we leave."

"May I have a drink, please?"

She indicated a bottle of champagne and a glass. She must have been bracing herself with it before they arrived. Dorange rose and filled the glass for her.

"Will you join me?"

"No, thanks."

It was becoming ridiculous. There was work to be done yet, and this woman, as usual, wished to make a party of it.

"What happened exactly after the cocktail party given at the *Carlton* to celebrate Vale's arrival?"

She drank, closed her eyes as she swallowed, and then opened them wide again. Just as though she might have been acting it under a film director's orders.

"Hal and I left the party, went up in the lift together, and he stepped out at the first floor. I preferred the second. You can see more of the sea and it's quiet. I insisted..."

"Vale left the lift at the first floor... Yes?"

"He wished to go up to my room with me. He suggested a private drink together. I said I was tired and begged him to leave me. That was the last time I saw him alive."

She sobbed and closed her eyes, and pressed her forefinger and thumb over her eyelids. It was like a close-up.

"I undressed and went to my bath. My maid had left me and I was alone. The telephone rang. It was Hal."

A pause for effect.

"He asked me to come down to his room right away, as he had something special to say to me. He sounded in distress and pleaded with me to go. I told him I was in my bath and I would go down as soon as I was able. I put on my bath-robe and then I quickly dressed. I went down the lift. His door was unlocked and a little open, as he said he would leave it so. When I entered the room there was nobody there. It is exactly like mine on the floor above it and I knew the room at the end with the light on was the bathroom. I spoke to him. There was no answer. I looked round the bathroom door..."

She closed her eyes and winced as though, in spite of it, she saw the fearful scene again.

"He was dead."

"How did you know?"

She looked at him in amazement, as she might have done to a member of an audience in a theatre who had questioned her in the middle of a scene on the stage.

"I knew it. He was crouching in the water, his eyes open wide and an awful grin on his face. As I looked at him, his body twitched and slid back in the water. It was like a nightmare. I ran to my room. My one thought was to get away... to get away to Paul."

"Why to Paul?"

"He is so superior to the rest. So far-seeing, so protective—so clever. I needed his advice and help."

"And he advised you to return?"

"Yes."

"So do I."

She twisted her fingers so tightly together that her knuckles turned white. It seemed to get on Dorange's nerves and, with a kindly smiling gesture, he placed his hand over hers and stilled them.

"You intended to marry Hal Vale?"

"It was not properly decided."

"Are you sure?"

She opened her eyes wide and raised her eyebrows, as though surprised at his doubting it.

"Of course. I had not made up my mind, although he had pressed me to agree."

Littlejohn rose and paced to the window. It was of double glass and soundproof. Below he could see reporters and photographers camped on the pavement in front, waiting. He turned quickly to Monique Dol.

"Was there any other man in the case?"

"Certainly not!"

The emphasis of the denial was suspicious. She was trying to hide something under a cloak of indignation.

"Why are you looking at me like that?"

"I'm not sure you're telling me the truth, Miss Dol. What was Mr. Armstrong to you?"

"A friend. He was interested in my acting. Our relations were purely business ones."

"I see."

"Do not be so hard on me, Superintendent. I assure you, I had nothing to do with the death of Hal Vale. I will do all I can to help you find out who killed him."

"Thank you. I hope you will."

"It was only panic made me run away. I was sure nobody would believe me. I wished to consult Paul."

"Did you consult him about marrying Hal Vale, or were matters undecided until you had done so?"

"Yes. They were. Paul has always been very good to me. Frankly, I am not always able to find work. Paul makes me a good allowance then. He is still my best friend. I wished to tell him that Hal had asked me to marry him..."

It was fantastic! Instead of falling in Vale's arms when he proposed to her, as she'd doubtless have done on the movies, she'd decided to ask her 'uncle' what he thought about the proposition! And perhaps ask how it would affect her allowance!

She took another glass of champagne, but it seemed to cast her down. Her mouth drooped at the corners. "I'm so miserable," she said. "So unhappy."

"How long was it between you and Vale leaving each other in the lift and your going to his room?"

"I would say about an hour."

"You met nobody on your way to or from Vale's bedroom?"

"No. But I think I heard the lift going down as I left my room."

"You have no more to tell me, Miss Dol?"

"No."

"Very well. I suggest you arrange to return to the Isle of Man right away."

She paused.

"Are you going to accompany me?"

It sounded like a coquettish invitation.

"You must excuse me. I have more work to do here. Besides, we don't wish to give the press the impression that I've arrested you, do we?"

They left her, now rushing round, packing, thrusting this and that indiscriminately in cases, flinging shoes and dresses about. Another act! When they had left, she'd probably ring for a maid and tell her to make a proper job of it!

Littlejohn had never fully explored Aix-en-Provence and Dorange, who was always ready for a quiet hour between spells of duty, took him in tow. There was a languid air about the old city as the two detectives loitered there through the hot afternoon, visiting antique shops, churches, open markets and public buildings, or lazily admiring the Cours Mirabeau and its splendid façades of one-time town houses of the old nobility of Provence. Now they were converted into hotels and apartment houses and flats, most of which had drawn shutters and the deserted look of homes whose owners have gone to the seaside. Then Littlejohn and Dorange sat under the trees, their drinks in front of them, watching the passers-by. Dusk fell and they were unable to shake off the charm of the old city and decided to stay the night. After booking rooms at the *Roy René*, they strolled out again under the trees in the half-light. They said little, each content in the other's company. Finally, they turned-in at their hotel for dinner.

Oeufs cocotte aux Truffes, Tournedos Grillé Béarnaise, Le pavé du Roy, came and went and they drank a *Châteauneuf du Pape* of a potency and weight which rarely goes for export.

Before he retired, Littlejohn rang the Isle of Man and asked for Knell. He made the call from the Commissariat at Aix, where he was received, on Dorange's introduction, with extraordinary honours and courtesy.

"Where are you speaking from, sir?"

"Aix-en-Provence, Knell."

"Where's that?"

"In Provence."

"Oh."

Knell had worked hard since Littlejohn left. He had interviewed every member of the film company, artists and technicians alike. The cocktail-party, which was concluding at the time Vale was murdered, provided a massive omnibus alibi for all except three of the party, two men and a girl, who had been enjoying the hospitality of the Island. The natives provided reputable confirmations.

Mr. Firmin, Vale's lawyer from London, was making himself a nuisance to the police. He seemed to think that he and they had failed in their duty of keeping Hal Vale alive! He had established himself at the *Carlton* and was on the 'phone almost every hour. "Any progress yet in the investigations?"

"When will you be back, sir?"

"Probably tomorrow morning's 'plane, Knell. Monique Dol was proposing to leave today and should be on the Island again tomorrow, although I wouldn't, if I were you, tell the film director yet. She's a bit vague in her plans and likely to change her mind."

It was then that Littlejohn thought it might be a good idea if they checked up at her flat in Maison Mauron, whether or not Monique had left.

It was dark as he and Dorange made their way again to the Cours Mirabeau. Lights shone in the trees and the many fountains of the boulevard splashed in the silence. Cafés were still open but mostly deserted. The annual musical festival had ended a few days ago. The university was closed for vacation and the students, who were their best customers, had gone. The law term was over, too, and the lawyers of the great legal centre were either away on holidays or at their week-end villas by the sea near Marseille.

Lights showed between the shutters of Monique Dol's flat as they approached the building.

"So she hasn't gone, Dorange."

The hall-porter, sleepily smoking a cigarette from which dangled a long pencil of ash, sprang to attention as they entered.

"Is Miss Dol still in her flat?"

"No, sir. She left shortly after you went."

"She spoke of leaving when we were here this morning. Has her luggage gone?"

"Yes, sir. I saw her and her luggage safely in M. Mauron's car, bound for Nice Airport."

The man took them up the lift and to the door of the flat. He knocked. There was no reply.

"You have a pass-key?"

"Yes. But..."

"Open it." said Dorange. The man obeyed.

All the lights were on in the salon and in the room beyond,

which from this morning's visit, they knew to be Monique Dol's bedroom.

Midway between the main door and the bedroom a body was stretched, face downwards, on the Aubusson carpet. A pool of blood had formed around the head and coagulated.

It was W. J. Armstrong. He was dead, and he had been shot through the throat.

6

THE INTRUDER

Dorange hurried to the telephone. This made it necessary for the porter, who had been hanging about wide-mouthed and wild-eyed, silently watching everything, to bestir himself. There was a private exchange in the hall. He hurried out without a word, ran all the way down the stairs, and plugged-in.

"*Allo!*"

"It's taken you long enough. Get me the police-station!"

"Police Headquarters? Dorange. Yes; Dorange. There's been a murder at the Maison Mauron... And send a doctor, too."

This was Dorange's case until the local police took over. He made the most of his brief authority. He gave a quick glance around the rooms, opened all the drawers, and went through Armstrong's pockets.

"There's nothing to show why Armstrong came here. Presumably he was in search of Monique for some reason. She, on the other hand, has cleared out. Someone was either waiting for Armstrong or called here and found him alone. I wonder if Monique has got back to England yet..."

Littlejohn took up the 'phone now.

At Nice airport they were able to tell him she had left on the early afternoon 'plane for London, which meant that, unless she decided to rest the night in London, she could now be back on the Isle of Man.

Littlejohn put through a call to Knell.

"Hello, sir. Still in Provence?"

"Yes. Any news, Knell?"

"Yes, sir. As far as the film unit's concerned, great news. Miss Dol's back. Arrived this evening. All the film-company turned out. Gave her a great reception.

"They've also signed on a Frenchman to take Hal Vale's place opposite Monique Dol in the film. Jean Bizot, he's called."

"That's all I want to know at present, old man. By the way, W. J. Armstrong's been murdered here tonight..."

The distant gasp was so intense that it sounded to come from across the street.

"Just make enquiries about anyone who might be missing from the film company, as a matter of routine. I'll be back tomorrow, I hope."

"Be glad to see you again, sir. I hope Mr. Kinrade's well and happy. And by the way, sir. A message came through for you tonight from Dublin police. Athlone have reported that a woman answering to the description of somebody called Clara Tebbs has been seen there. They're investigating."

Clara Tebbs! She seemed part of another world and Littlejohn had forgotten all about her.

"Telephone through to Cromwell at The Yard, will you? Tell him what's happened, and ask him to speak to Dublin. Thanks, old man."

Littlejohn turned to Dorange, who was sitting smoking a cigarette with his feet on a chair.

"Monique had a perfect alibi. She's on the Isle of Man."

Downstairs in the hall, the porter was smoking a cigarette, too, wondering whether or not to return upstairs. He was bewildered, as he'd heard no shot, seen no intruder, not even known that all the lights were on in Monique Dol's flat. The reception department was luxurious, like everything else. Marble floor and stairs, mahogany desk for the receptionist, which the porter was now occupying, gilded gates for the lifts, palms in pots at each corner.

The police arrived with the doctor. Two plain-clothes men and one in uniform. The doctor was small and dark and carried a bag. He had a face like a greyhound.

"He's on the first floor, stone dead," said the porter who'd listened-in to Dorange's telephone-call. "I'll take you up."

He might have been doing them a favour!

Brief introductions, and the policemen spread themselves, two busy with the corpse, the third taking notes from Dorange. The doctor knelt beside the body and spread the contents of his bag around him as though he were going to wire-in and perform an autopsy on the spot.

"Ring for the police vehicle and we'll move the body as soon as we can," he said, as he examined what was left of W. J. Armstrong cursorily. "We'd better get him out of the way as soon as possible. Monsieur Mauron wouldn't like the body hanging about in this flat."

At the mention of the name, the inspector in charge looked alarmed and nodded earnestly. It was evident that Mauron was a power in the land here, too.

The porter was back.

"They'll be here any minute. As soon as I mentioned that it was in Monsieur Mauron's flat, you could hear them start bustling about."

"How long has he been dead?"

Dorange seemed to think it time they changed the subject. The doctor squatted back on his heels.

"I'd say between two and four hours..."

"Can't you be more precise?"

"Not here, Inspector. I'll be able to make a closer estimate after we've got at him and performed a proper post-mortem examination."

The local inspector was on the telephone again. This time to the Procureur. He'd gone right to the top because the case involved Paul Mauron.

"You'll excuse me troubling you, M. le Procureur, but it's a murder in the flat of Monsieur Paul Mauron..."

The Procureur was out at a dinner party and would have ticked-off the officer for bothering him with an ordinary murder in such circumstances. A subordinate could have done the job. But now you could hear him shouting instructions.

"Hold everything until I arrive. No press, no photographs. Deal with it all discreetly. I'll come myself..."

The ambulance was there. Two men, looking as if they'd been suddenly wakened from their beds, shuffled in with a stretcher and, remembering it was the flat of Monsieur Mauron, removed their caps.

"You'd better leave the body as it is until the Procureur arrives," the police inspector told them.

The two men looked bewildered and didn't know how to spend their waiting time. Finally, they retired to the lobby for a smoke.

A fresh arrival. A dapper little man in a dinner jacket. His shoes were of shining patent leather, he was swarthy, and his hair was plastered down sleekly with brilliantine. He looked like a band leader.

"What do *you* want and who are you?"

The local inspector thought it was time to show his authority.

"I'm manager of the flats. The hall-porter informed me—it's his duty—there's been a murder here. Very inconvenient. I was at dinner. I don't know what Monsieur Mauron will say."

Another! Dorange was getting a bit rattled.

"Now that you've been informed and seen the body... there it is... I suggest you go back to your dinner. We don't want any more people roaming about here. Good evening."

The man's mouth opened and shut and then, mustering all the dignity he could, he strode from the room, breathing hard.

"I shall report to Monsieur Mauron that the police..."

"Tell him what you like. And enjoy what's left of your dinner."

The lift was whining again. The clang of gates, and then two more men. One was tall and heavy, with an ivory complexion and a bald head. He also was in evening clothes, but of a more elegant cut than those of the manager of the flats. He wore a monocle which he screwed in his eye on ceremonial occasions when he wasn't with his wife, who detested it. His companion was smaller, thick-set, cleanshaven, thin on top, bespectacled, fussy. The Procureur de la Republique and one of the examining magistrates. They were talking together as they entered. The elder man's voice was sharp and decisive, that of one used to ordering people about. Except, of course, his wife. The other scuttered here and there like a beetle in a bottle, but he hardly spoke. *Oui, Monsieur le Procureur. Non, Monsieur le Procureur. Mais certainement, Monsieur le Procureur...*

More introductions. The Procureur was intrigued to know what Dorange was doing there, a member of the Sûreté of Nice. It almost amounted to poaching on another's preserves!

Explanations. Congratulations. Felicitations to Littlejohn.

"I'm sure that Monsieur Mauron will be glad that matters are in such good hands."

Not again! The Procureur this time, too!

"It is very embarrassing for such a thing to happen here. Monsieur Mauron will be very upset about it, I'm sure. However, we must do our best. Discretion and good taste, eh, gentlemen? Monsieur Hauteroche!"

"Oui, Monsieur le Procureur."

"You may proceed."

"Merci, Monsieur le Procureur."

The examining magistrate opened his brief-case and started to look businesslike.

More of them! This time the members of the Parquet. Specialists, photographers, scribes, fingerprint experts.

"Treat the premises with respect, gentlemen. Monsieur Mauron..."

"*Mais certainement, Monsieur le Procureur.*"

And they all set to work. The fingerprint staff took those of W. J. Armstrong for a start and then the two men were called to carry off the body to the medico-legal laboratory, which was in the cemetery. They had been having a drink to while away the time and compassionately breathed alcohol over the corpse.

A reporter who had tacked himself on the rear of the procession was recognised and kicked out, and a press-photographer who had insinuated himself among the cameras of the Parquet was identified and ejected.

Meanwhile, Dorange was interrogating the hall-porter. This man had an easy job. His chief function was to act as an ornament at the entrance to the flats, to open the door of cars calling there, and to make short work of all nuisances who might annoy the tenants. He had been, until age caught up with him, a cycling champion who had won the Tour de France in his youth. He had now gone to seed and was tall, paunchy, pear-shaped and slow and he wore a large moustache of which he was very proud. He had been born on the waterfront of Marseille, the illegitimate son of a washerwoman.

"After we left here at noon, did Miss Dol depart right away?"

"Yes. As I said before, I saw her off."

"Any telephone messages for her, in or out?"

"No, sir."

"Any visitors?"

"Again no, sir."

"How, then, did the dead man get in the flat? Not by climbing in the window from a helicopter! Think again. You say you didn't see him go up to the flat. Have you been out since Miss Dol left?"

"I always have my meals in the room at the back, with the door open so I can see anybody who enters by the front one."

He blew a blast of garlic over Dorange, who recoiled.

"Surely, in a block like this, there's someone coming and going all the time."

"Yes, sir. But I always know who they're visiting. Tradesmen, of course, always go round to the rear."

"Do they go up to the flats from the back with their goods?"

"Some of them. Personal messages and the like, must be delivered to the persons themselves; the rest, they leave me to deliver."

"There's no porter at the back to check who comes and goes?"

"No. But the door is always locked. It's like this. If a tradesman or messenger wants to deliver anything that's to go in by the back, he rings the bell and I go and let him in."

"And whilst you're absent, someone might come in by the front, climb the stairs without your seeing him, and get to one of the flats without being detected?"

"I'm never away above a couple of minutes."

"But that could happen."

"I suppose so."

"Was the flat locked after Miss Dol left for Nice?"

"Yes, sir. I went up to see the lights were off and the place safe and straight. Then I snapped the door to. It's a spring lock."

"Who has the keys?"

The porter smiled and looked very magnanimous.

"Well, sir, anybody who wants to sleep in the place. Monsieur Mauron doesn't occupy it much and if he's not in residence, he likes his friends to use it if they need it."

"Who are these friends?"

"Miss Dol's one. She has a key. Mr. Armstrong had one, too. He used to stay the night when he was in Aix. Mr. Hal Vale had one... I guess Monsieur Mauron's handed out dozens of 'em from time to time with invitations to his friends to make themselves at home here."

"Have you a list of these people?"

"No, sir. I'd have to think a long time to recollect all the people that have been in this flat for long and short stays. I will say that Monsieur Mauron always insisted on people writing to the agent beforehand to let him know they were coming, so we could air the place and put linen on the bed and the like. I'll think of their names, sir, and make you a list."

"Are all the flats here occupied?"

"Yes, sir. They're in big demand. But a lot of the tenants are at present away on holidays. There's five flats, and six of the tenants are away."

"Has Miss Dol had any visitors lately?"

"Not since she arrived two days ago."

"So, you neither saw the man who's been killed, nor his killer."

"I swear I didn't."

"No need to swear. I believe you. Does Monsieur Mauron come here to stay often?"

"Sometimes for the odd night. He's not been here lately. I guess we'll have to let him know about all this."

"Do *you* do it?"

"No. M. Audriffet does it."

"Who's he?"

"The flats manager. He's employed by the firm of agents for the property and does this job part-time. He telephones Monsieur Mauron when there's any message or emergency."

"Even when he's at sea on his yacht?"

"Yes. By radio-telephone, then."

"Get M. Mauron on the radio-telephone."

"But..."

"Get him."

The man was not long about it. The national telephone was

soon linked with Mauron's yacht through the radio station at Grasse.

"Mauron speaking. Who is it?"

"Dorange. Nice Sûreté."

"Well, Inspector? Did you see Miss Dol, as arranged?"

"Yes, sir. I'm telephoning to tell you that my colleagues and I are at your flat in Aix now. Miss Dol left just after noon, but Mr. Armstrong has been found here, shot dead."

"When?"

"About three hours ago according to the doctor."

"I see. Is Miss Dol all right?"

"Yes. She is already back on the Isle of Man."

"Very well. Please telephone me tomorrow and report developments."

Mauron was as cool as a cucumber. No dismay; not even regrets. Dorange might have been telephoning the results of a football match!

"I'm not on the case, sir. I just happened to call with Superintendent Littlejohn. The Aix police will be in charge."

"Then, tell Leblanc de Montvallon, the Procureur, to keep in touch with me. Tell him, if needed, he must not hesitate to ask for more help from the Sûreté at Marseille. Thank you for this cooperation and for informing me. I will not forget it."

Dorange smiled to himself. He felt if Mauron had been physically on the spot he might have given him a tip!

"May I ask you a question, sir?"

"Certainly."

"Who is Mr. W. J. Armstrong, the murdered man?"

"He is my agent in England. His headquarters are at the London office of the banking house of Mauron and Berluc-Pertussis, of Marseille."

"Where are you now, sir?"

A pause.

"Anchored off Messina."

"Thank you, sir."

"Don't forget. Instruct Leblanc de Montvallon to keep me informed."

That was a good one! Dorange smiled grimly. Mauron instructing le Procureur de la Republique to keep him informed!

When he passed on Mauron's message to the Procureur, M. Leblanc seemed flattered. He promised without more ado to contact Mauron every day until the case was solved.

"As for calling in help from Marseille. I think, Inspector, we of Aix can manage very well ourselves. Were Monsieur Mauron here, I would not hesitate to tell him so."

Dorange wished Mauron would suddenly materialise for the purpose!

Later, at their hotel, Dorange and Littlejohn discussed the case until the early hours of the morning.

What had Armstrong been up to at Maison Mauron?

Had he merely made a call there hoping to find Monique Dol and had his killer caught up with him?

Had he any particular reason, beyond friendship, for calling on Monique? Some people talked of his being in love with her. Had he followed her to press his case now that Hal Vale was out of the running? Or...

And here Littlejohn, fresh from the background of the Isle of Man and the atmosphere of the *Carlton* in Douglas, had one of his hunches.

"Could it be that on her way to Vale's bedroom, Monique Dol saw someone coming away... someone who might have been Vale's murderer?"

"In that case, the murderer would have been out to kill Monique, not Armstrong, don't you think?"

"That's it. Perhaps she saw Armstrong. But he never had a chance to deal with her alone. She fled at once to Cannes. Is that why she ran away to Mauron—for protection? Armstrong followed, caught up with her in Aix, but there encountered some bodyguard or other Mauron had provided."

"It's quite possible, but how are we to find out? No use questioning Mauron, Littlejohn. He's hardly likely to give away one of his own operators. Mauron himself and Monique have alibis; one on the Isle of Man, the other at Messina..."

"It looks as if I'd better return to the Island right away and tackle Monique again. Meanwhile, the Aix police will pursue the local murder in their own way."

They left it at that and slept on it.

The only obstacle to Littlejohn's immediate return to the Isle of Man was the Rev. Caesar Kinrade. He was in Nice at the flower farm of the Dorange family and was greatly enjoying himself. A pity to cut short his holiday. The problem was quickly solved, however. Over the telephone, the Archdeacon expressed his decision to stay at Nice for a while, after Littlejohn had assured him that, on the Manx side of the case, he would find it much more convenient to make his headquarters at the *Carlton* than at Grenaby vicarage. He arranged to catch the ten o'clock 'plane from Marseille to Paris, and thence fly direct to Manchester and the Island.

"We'll keep an eye on Mauron and the rest of them for you," promised Dorange. "Already, I expect, Mauron's on his way back to Aix by air. Full details will have reached him wherever he is now, and he's not likely to leave the problems of Monique and Armstrong to stew in their own juice."

"I still can't think what Armstrong was doing in Monique's flat."

"All the Mauron gang come and go in these parts. It's their headquarters, here and in Cannes. Armstrong, Monique, Vale, Marie Vale, his third wife, Firmin, McLeary... To quote only a few characters connected with the case. They've all been here recently according to the list of visitors compiled from memory for me by the hall-porter. And, he tells me, they've all got a key to the place.

Mauron distributes keys liberally to all his friends who might use the flat. They come and go, and the local police keep an eye on them."

"Firmin?"

"Guy Firmin. Vale's lawyer and business man. And Joe McLeary, his advertising agent."

"And Marie, the third wife... Let's see, she was the wife of a fellow called de Beer before she divorced him?"

"Yes. De Beer is dead. The divorce between Marie and Vale is still not absolute in the English courts. Unless he's already altered his will, she'll inherit his fortune. And, I gather, Vale was a rich man. He had a knack of saving his money and preying or sponging on other people. Mauron must have helped him quite a lot in his time. Vale had been poor and knew the value of money. He'd no intention of being poverty-stricken again. His kind can fall from grace and easy money almost overnight. It's well-known that Vale knew how to look after his money."

"There's motive there. If Mrs. Vale the Third stood to lose a fortune as soon as the divorce became absolute, she might well have thought of dropping an electric razor in Hal's bath."

"She was in Nice, however, when Hal was murdered. She's a perfect alibi. She was invited to make a trip to Greece with Mauron. When the news about Vale came, she crossed to London right away. Before you arrived."

"You seem to have a lot of information about Vale and his connections, Dorange."

"You must remember, Vale and his retinue spent a lot of spare time on the Côte d'Azur, Littlejohn. They were more in France than in England. We keep large dossiers about such people. Sometimes, they overstep the line between right and wrong. And also, they were tied-up with Mauron. We know quite a lot about *him*. In fact, he might be surprised and upset if he knew the whole of what we know."

"Was Vale good to his ex-wives?"

"He remained friends with all of them, if that's what you mean. If you're referring to his generosity to them after he'd finished with them, that's another matter. I've already told you, he was careful with his money. He seems to have settled on them just enough for them to live in comfort. Two of them, of course, remarried and are well-off. Marie, unless she, too, had found another wealthy husband to support her, would probably have been dependent on friends like Mauron for the luxuries of life."

Littlejohn and Dorange were sitting in the breakfast-room of the *Roy René*. Littlejohn was loath to go. He'd have preferred a little more of France and the company of his good friend.

Dorange seemed to read his thoughts.

"Never mind, my friend. Come back again when it's all over."

"According to local gossip around Nice, would you say that Vale and Monique would soon have married?"

"I don't know. It's common knowledge that Vale was crazy about her. But she, somehow, hadn't made up her mind. That was the talk of the Nice hotels, where divorcees, dowagers, widows, and the waiting-ones foregather. There seems to have been no question of anyone else with Monique. She simply seemed to be long in making up her mind."

"Perhaps Mauron hadn't given his consent!"

"I believe he's quite complacent about such things. Whoever Monique marries or divorces, he still remains *mon oncle* to her."

"Did Marie Vale spend her time pending her divorce among those you call the waiting-ones?"

"Mostly."

"Did Vale still meet her?"

"Not as far as I know. They remained friends, it was said, but during the formalities of the divorce, Guy Firmin was the go-between. He attended to the legal matters. Have you met him?"

"Not yet. I hear he's on the Isle of Man, pestering the police for results."

"He's a bachelor. Vale's handy-man. The one who used to get

him out of his minor scrapes with women and film companies. Between his marriages, Vale was promiscuous. Small-part actresses, local *cocottes*, sometimes even a waitress, a lady's-maid, a flower-seller, or a cinema usherette... Firmin sorted it all out."

"Did he deal, too, with Monique and Marie?"

"No doubt he put the legal, the settlement side of the proposals to both of them. He is adept. Probably also he took care of Vale's fortune. His man of affairs. Firmin seems to do very well out of it and lives very comfortably. No doubt, those he encounters, such as Mauron, have been in the habit of putting him on money-making schemes. That gang make the habit of giving each other all the latest tips for the stock exchanges of the world. They are the close corporation which stands behind much of the finance of every capital city."

"By the way, is Marie French, too?"

"No, she's Irish by birth. Marie Doyle was her maiden name."

The changes for Littlejohn were, after that, quick ones. The shady boulevards of Aix, the busy city and airport of Marseille, the swift flight of the *Caravelle* across the mountains of Provence. Paris, Manchester, Ronaldsway...

Knell was waiting for him. His pleasure was good to see.

"Where's the Rev. Caesar, sir?"

"He's stayed on with his friends in Nice."

Knell laughed.

"That's something new for the pazon. He's always talking about taking a holiday. He even packs his bags and orders his taxi for the airport. Then, he decides there's no place in the world half so nice as his dear li'l Island, and, at the last minute, he cancels all his arrangements and stays at home."

"Any developments at this end, Knell?"

"No clues, no theories, if that's what you mean, sir. The film unit's still at the *Carlton* and the return of Monica Dol's been a tonic to them. They threw a big party last night and they're going on location again tomorrow. The new French star in place of Vale is here handing out autographs. The news that W. J. Armstrong had been murdered came as a bit of a shock to one or two of them, but it seems the financial part of the business will go on very well without him. Miss Dol fainted when they broke the news, but she's recovered, thanks, it's said, to the sympathy shown her by her fellow countryman, Jean Bizot..."

"This case is very involved... very widespread, isn't it?"

"Yes, sir. Very involved. There are two hundred people staying at the *Carlton*. I guess almost any one of them could have sneaked up to Vale's room and tossed a razor in his bath. Plenty of alibis. Too many, if you ask me."

"You've interviewed all the staff?"

"Yes. I've a book full of interviews. I'll show it to you when we get to the police-station."

Over the fairy-bridge at Ballalona, where they raised their hats to propitiate the little people. Back to the unsophisticated old ways again. What a relief! Knell, as usual, felt that help from any source, natural or supernatural, was going to be needed before this case was finished! Then along the quiet roads to Douglas, where they made a halt at headquarters.

Knell had made a thorough job of the details of the investigation. He'd combed the streets surrounding the *Carlton* and questioned hotel staffs, porters, cabbies, hawkers, barmen, owners of sideshows and shops. Even officials in a nearby branch bank.

Notices had been posted in the halls of hotels, pubs and boarding-houses. *Information Required by the Police.* Comings and goings at the side entrances of the *Carlton*. Suspicious characters, strange behaviour, unusual goings-on... Not a solitary piece of useful information, but a huge mail of letters from would-be helpers, busybodies, and crackpots. Some had even reported at length on the arrival of the police at the side door and the departure of the late Hal Vale by the luggage entrance.

Then a careful time-table of all that had gone on at the *Carlton* around the time of Hal Vale's death.

Vale's 'plane arrives I.O.M.....2.00

Vale and Miss Dol arrive at Carlton Hotel.....3.30

Cocktail party.....4.00

Vale and M. Dol retire.....4.15

Vale rings for valet.....5.00

Valet arrives Vale's room.....5.10

Valet leaves Vale's room.....5.30

Valet returns and finds Vale.....6.30

W. J. Armstrong rings M. Dol.....6.45

M.Dol in Vale's room (finds him dead).....5.40 (?)

M.Dol catches London 'plane from airport.....6.30

Littlejohn looked at his wrist-watch. Half-past four. As he did so, a small sports car drew up at the police station. There was some conversation in the office outside and a cheerful bobby put his head in at the door of Knell's room.

"Mr. Firmin again."

Littlejohn felt he'd had enough. The sudden change from the South of France to the Isle of Man and the switching from one aspect of the case to another atmosphere altogether had bewildered him a bit. He felt he'd rather take a walk along the promenade, mix with the visitors, enjoy the holiday feeling again. Instead...

"Show him in."

Another tall, lean man. This time he didn't sport a monocle, but he was true to the type of the Mauron set. Well-dressed in a suit of expensive flannel, smart tie and linen, easy manners, obviously a man of the world. One who took good care of himself, too. Massage, sun-lamps, well-shaved and manicured, smelling slightly of male cosmetics. He was middle-aged, with tired, dark, heavy-lidded eyes, a large Roman nose, and a firm square chin.

"I hear Superintendent Littlejohn is back from France."

The international pigeon-post had been at it again! Probably Firmin knew all about Monique Dol's escapades, the death of W. J. Armstrong, and a lot more as well. Perhaps he even knew who'd killed Armstrong.

Littlejohn was beginning to feel that he himself was the criminal and Mauron and his extensive network were on his trail!

7
AT THE CARLTON AGAIN

Firmin extended a strong, well-kept hand at Littlejohn, who shook it. It was hot and dry. There was a large signet-ring with a carved stone on the little finger.

"I've called, as usual, to ask if there's any more news about Vale's case. Inspector Knell will tell you that it's now become a part of my daily routine."

He nodded and smiled at Knell, who frowned back at him to let him know that his importunities were doing no good at all.

"Sit down, Mr. Firmin. I'd like to ask you some questions."

Firmin chose the most comfortable chair of a motley assembly and crossed his legs languidly.

"Anything I can do to help, Superintendent? How did you find Cannes and Aix?"

"Very pleasant, thanks. I expect you already know that W. J. Armstrong was shot dead in Aix last night."

"As a matter of fact, I do. Paul Mauron got there by air just after noon."

Of course. That went without saying. Trust Mauron.

"Who told you all this?"

"Mauron's secretary."

"Have you any idea who might have killed Armstrong?"

"Your guess is as good as mine."

"How long have you been on the Island, Mr. Firmin?"

"I arrived by first 'plane on the morning after Hal's death."

"You were in London at the time of the crime, I hear."

"Yes. Am I supposed to provide an alibi?"

"I'm not asking you for one, but, as a lawyer, you'll know the advantage of having one."

"I gather Hal Vale met his death between five-thirty and six-thirty. I was in London at the time, alone in my flat. I left to join friends at a night-club around nine o'clock. The news of Hal's death reached me almost immediately I arrived at the club. That's as far as I can go."

"And nobody saw you in your flat or on your way to the night club? Which night club, by the way?"

"Nobody I could call on for an alibi. The night-club was *The Winking Light* in Frith Street. You know it? It's called after the flashing lights of the pedestrian crossing outside."

"Thank you. Had Hal Vale any enemies who might have...?"

"Wished to murder him? Certainly not."

Firmin said it light-heartedly. It might have been a joke.

"I can assure you that he *was* murdered. Who, then, could have wished him out of the way?"

"I can't think. I'm stumped."

"Vale was a wealthy man?"

"Yes; he not only earned a lot on the films, but had a flair for making money. He speculated on the Stock Exchange. That hasn't been difficult of late and he certainly cashed-in on recent markets."

"What about his will? Who are the beneficiaries?"

"Rather premature, aren't you, Superintendent?"

"No, sir. It will soon be public property anyway. In the circumstances there's no harm in telling the police now. It may help us a lot."

"I guess you're right and, as a lawyer, I ought to assist you. Vale made a new will when he married Marie de Beer. He always did on such occasions. He left modest legacies to certain relatives. His aged father is still alive and lives with two of Vale's aunts at Blackpool. There's a string of bequests to some of his intimates, too, including me. Nothing to shout about. Mine's an odd thousand. Then, similar amounts to some of his film friends. People who, we might say, were dependent on Vale's charity, were remembered. The residue, a substantial one, too, goes to Marie, his third wife..."

"What about the two previous wives?"

"They are already married again to rich men. Their alimony is the subject of certain trusts which will continue. He left them nothing in his will. Marie would have been the same had he lived a week longer. Already, I have a new draft will in my office, cutting-out Marie as soon as the decree becomes absolute. She would then benefit under an alimony trust yielding a much smaller income altogether."

"And as soon as he married Monique Dol, he'd make another will in Monique's favour?"

"Yes. Their marriage would have taken place almost at once after the decree with Marie became absolute."

"Marie, I gather, was divorcing Vale."

"Yes. That was always the case with Hal Vale. He'd nothing much with which to reproach his wives."

"Had Marie Vale any plans for marrying again when she was free of Vale?"

"Not as far as I know. I'm sure I'd know if she had."

Littlejohn was sure, too. Nothing seemed to go on anywhere without the members of the gang knowing it.

"Did you know W. J. Armstrong well, Mr. Firmin?"

Firmin yawned. He looked bored as though he'd had enough.

"Pretty well. He's financed certain of Vale's films and I've had quite a bit to do with him on the legal side. Why?"

"Can you suggest what he was doing in Aix when he met his death?"

"Probably calling on Monique. He'd taken quite a fancy to her. Sent her flowers and was always ringing her up. Perhaps he was in love with her, but he was the solemn, grim type. A controlled kind of man who never wore his heart on his sleeve. You don't think *he* killed Vale?"

Littlejohn remembered Paul Mauron's disgust at the idea of *crime passionnel*. He and his friends, including Monique, were supposed to be too civilised, too sophisticated to indulge in heroics, however much they might act in films about them.

"To use your own words, Mr. Firmin—your guess is as good as mine."

"What do you make of it all, Superintendent? Or am I not supposed to ask?"

"I don't make anything of it yet, sir."

Outside, the sounds of holiday-making were beginning to die down. People were on their way home to high teas and a string of charabancs passed taking sightseers back to their lodgings. Littlejohn's eyes kept falling on the hoarding opposite on which the season's attractions were advertised.

The Desmond Horla Show. Featuring Desmond Horla.
Johnny Weems and his Orchestra. The Beat Boys.
Marathon Dancing at Villa Marina.
Skiffle Group Contest...

It all looked very alien in the world in which Littlejohn and Knell were entangled and getting precious few results.

"Is that all?"

"I think so, for the time being. Are any members of the film unit returning to London tomorrow? I hear the inquest on Vale was held earlier today and the funeral is at Golder's Green tomorrow."

"Yes. Some will be going, including myself. Monique won't be there. She says she can't stand it. Any objection to our leaving for the day?"

"No, provided we can find anyone we need."

"I can assure you of that. Inspector Knell's sewn it all up."

"I'll keep in touch with you then, Mr. Firmin. Is Mr. McLeary crossing to England tomorrow, too?"

"Yes. He's several matters to see to as well as the cremation."

"I'd better have a word with him before he leaves."

"I'll tell him you wish to see him, then. Is that all?"

"I take it Miss Dol is at the *Carlton*."

"Yes; she's back in her old room, I believe."

"Good-bye then..."

Littlejohn and Knell looked blankly at one another when he'd gone.

"What do you make of it all, old chap?"

"They all seem to have alibis, sir. McLeary was off the Island, too, when the murder occurred. He was in Blackpool, arranging the première of Vale's latest film."

"Let's run along to the *Carlton* and see him."

The town and promenade were deserted as the pair of them made their way to the hotel. Everybody was in for high tea or preparing for dinner. Even the sea seemed to be taking a rest. Deep blue, like a sheet of glass, with tired little waves flapping about on the ebb tide. A horse-tram with only a couple of passengers aboard passed them and then a landau drawn by a leisurely old horse and carrying a load of elderly heavy people, who seemed to be having a good time.

McLeary was expecting them in the lounge. A little, stocky Irishman with the face of an ex-pugilist and light hair clipped close to his skull to make his baldness less conspicuous.

"Firmin said you wanted me. What about a drink? Now, don't say you're on duty. I won't accept that as an excuse. Come along."

"First of all, Mr. McLeary, is Miss Dol available?"

"We'll see..."

McLeary picked up one of the telephones in the hall and asked for Monique Dol's room. There was a brief conversation.

"She's dressing for dinner and has just got out of her bath..."

McLeary smiled grimly. Littlejohn knew what he was thinking. After what Monique had found in Vale's bath only a few days ago, it was a wonder she could face her own for some time to come! But there it was...

"Will you kindly tell her, I'll be back later this evening to see her, Mr. McLeary? Say, nine o'clock."

"What if she's engaged or busy?"

"I also am busy, Mr. McLeary. I've already chased her all over Europe and back to no purpose. I'm doing no more running or waiting for Miss Dol. I shall be here at nine and I expect her to be available. Will you please tell her that?"

McLeary roared with laughter.

"Will I tell her? You betya I will. I wouldn't miss that for anything. Imagine anybody telling Monique what to do. I'll love to see her face. Can I tell her you'll arrest her if she isn't here on nine?"

"Don't go so far, Mr. McLeary. Just my message, please."

There was a big crowd in the bar and everybody was talking at once. A general atmosphere of jubilation at resumption of the film work. They were mostly members of the film unit and their friends. The celebrated comedian was there, too, with another celebrated comedian who was appearing in a show at the *Palace*. The first celebrated comedian was loud in his complaints. His part had been cut out of the film.

"I've turned down at least a dozen offers from seaside resorts this summer to appear in this film, and look where it's landed me. It's not damn well good enough."

He seemed to have lost his sense of humour altogether. At the best of times, it was phoney.

Littlejohn and his companions sat in a corner.

"What'll it be?"

"*Pernod*."

Knell's eyes opened wide. What was that?

"Me, too."

The barman had to dust the bottle for them.

People kept eyeing Littlejohn, some of them suspiciously, as though, at any moment, he was going to arrest someone. Newsmen tried to get at him now and then, but McLeary gave them short shrift.

"He's entitled to his drink in peace, like anybody else."

Now that they'd run McLeary to earth, Littlejohn didn't know what to ask him. The same old question about Hal Vale having any enemies, his wives, and the alibis of McLeary and the rest. He got the same answers. McLeary, like Firmin, had been changing to go to a party at the time Vale met his death. It seemed to be a perpetual round of parties, motor rides, yachting trips, excursions to the Mediterranean, cocktail bars... As though everyone connected with Hal Vale couldn't bear to be alone for a minute.

"You were staying in Blackpool?"

"Lytham. The *Clifton* Arms."

"You were there changing between five and six?"

"I had a conference with the cinema people about Hal's première in a fortnight. I left them at four o'clock, got to Lytham at half-past, had a bath, changed, had a drink in my room, and left for the party at seven. Why? You don't think I'd kill Hal, do you? He was my bread-and-butter. Like hell he was!"

That was right. Hal had been bread-and-butter for most of the people staying at the *Carlton*. Actors, technicians, hangers-on, and, of course, his personal staff, like Firmin and McLeary. But a lot of Vale's intimates would turn up their noses at bread-and-butter. They wanted champagne and oysters, expensive cars, yachts, women in mink coats. Suppose Vale's death meant all these to someone or other.

"I hear Marie Vale is staying here."

"Yes. She's out. A London dressmaker has crossed and is seeing her at one of the hotels about her clothes for the funeral. It's tomorrow."

"You know her well?"

"Yes. I should do, shouldn't I? I'm the man who gives the gossip writers all the dope about her and the rest. She's a very decent sort, is Marie. I said when he married her, it wouldn't last. She's not the kind for this hothouse film world. She's a lady born. Rubbed shoulders with the real people when her first husband was in the diplomatic service. I guess she'll go back to her own world again, now."

McLeary tossed back his brandy-and-soda.

"Another?"

"No, thanks. We'd better be getting along."

McLeary ordered himself another drink. He didn't seem disposed to move. Passers-by kept greeting him and looking keenly at the detectives. The comedian was still complaining.

"You're a friend of Firmin?"

"Business, that's all. We met a lot arranging Hal's affairs. He's not in my class. Needs a bit of keeping up with. A man of expensive tastes. Firmin moves among the people who make the easy money and spend it freely..."

Again. Easy money!

"W. J. Armstrong. What of him, Mr. McLeary?"

"Call me Joe. Armstrong, did you say? Pity he went and got himself killed, just as he was getting near what he wanted. Between you and me, he's been mad about Monique Dol for years. Always offering to finance a film for her. Now, when he's got his wish, he goes and stops a bullet. Some people are unlucky, aren't they?"

"He was a rival of Hal Vale's?"

"Well, hardly. I don't think Monique cared a button for Armstrong, except that he was in the money and a friend of her former husband, Paul Mauron. Monique had queer tastes in men, you see. She liked the older ones, but not as lovers, if you get me. She wanted them to confide in, to make life smooth for her, to find her money when she was hard-up. And she *was* hard-up, often. She spends money like water. No idea of values, you see. The day before Hal died, I saw her give a fiver to a chap with a donkey and cart. Told him the donkey looked hungry and to go and buy it a square meal. The bloke whipped up his moke and was off like a shot before she realised how much she'd given him..."

"And Armstrong?"

"Oh, yes. W. J. He was in love with her, I think. Only he was the silent sort, held his feelings on a tight rein. They're the worst kind, you know. I'm sure he followed her to the south of France as soon as he knew she'd got there."

"Perhaps he killed Vale to prevent his marrying Monique Dol."

"He might have had an alibi. But we'll never know now, will we?"

Knell waved his empty glass as he said it. The barman had filled it up for him again and what Knell initially thought tasted like harmless cough-linctus was now proving to be a mixture of quite another sort. As he was feeling now, he was sure he could cope with any of *that lot*, as he called the Vale group.

"Sure, he had an alibi, Mr. Knell. Sure. Even if he'd done it, Armstrong would have had an alibi. He was that sort."

The brandy was beginning to work on Joe McLeary, making him talkative, lowering his guard.

"Miss Dol seemed to have some hesitation about finally deciding to marry Hal Vale, Joe. Am I right?"

"Sure."

"Why?"

Joe had another fill-up and waved his glass airily as he spoke.

"There was a bit of bother about this film on the Island. Finance, you see. Monique's not been very lucky over her last film or two. The money's been tight, and only at the last minute has she been able to persuade somebody, through the influence of

Paul Mauron, to put up the cash. I know all this because it's my business as publicity man to the group. Her last film was a bit of a financial flop. Matter of fact, Paul Mauron advised her to chuck it. She always thinks she's the only one in the film. Quarrelling with directors and other actors... Folks'll only take so much and then they dig their heels in and won't play... Oh, I know you'll say she's lovely, charming... all that. But that's part of her act. On location, she's a devil. Hard as nails. Well, it boiled down to her wanting to have a film company of her own. She persuaded Hal Vale to put up the cash. Hal, of course, was careful with his money. But this time, he'd got it bad about Monique. He was mad about her. If he didn't put up the lolly, W. J. Armstrong would. So Monique won. Hal was going to form a company and provide the capital."

"I see. I believe he'd plenty."

"I'll say he had."

"Invested in gilt-edged?"

"Not on your life. Most of Hal's cash was in one or another of Paul Mauron's companies. Mauron's a banker, you know, when he cares to work, and he's a very skilled financier. A millionaire over and over again. He was Hal's financial adviser and made a fortune for him."

"I see. And Hal was going to use it to finance Monique's films."

"That's it. He must have loved her! Nothing short of something of that sort would separate Hal and his money."

"Have you and Firmin been on the Isle of Man before, Joe?"

"Changing the subject, are you, Super? Must confess it relieves me. Hal's finances are confidential, you know. You were saying...? Me and Firmin? We've not been here till we flew over ahead of the film company. We had to see to Hal's accommodation; or rather, I had. And the publicity, too. Had to let the world know where he was coming. Firmin had one or two legal points to attend to. We came a few days before the rest."

"You stayed here?"

"Naturally. Why?"

"I just wondered."

McLeary said good-bye to them on the hotel steps. A reporter buttonholed him as he turned to go.

"Those the police? Anything fresh, Joe?"

Littlejohn felt he'd rather go hungry than dine among the milling crowds at the *Carlton*. The day's news had revitalised everybody. Those who had packed their bags ready for off, had unpacked them again. The well-known members of the cast had recovered their pride and were parading here and there, giving autographs and showing-off in front of strangers. Technicians, saved from another flop and glad to be back at work, were drinking each other's health.

"Let's have a quiet meal somewhere."

Knell took him to a homely hotel at Derbyhaven. No film-stars there, no luxury yachtsmen, or international financiers. The quiet bay with the tide gently coming in, children playing on the shore among the rocks and seaweed, earnest men lost in contemplating their own little boats, or else tinkering with them. A peaceful meal with none of the ritual nonsense of a fashionable hotel. The healthy, appetising air of a country restaurant, a fine nicely garnished steak, apple pie and cream, and some good cheese to follow. The manager appeared quietly now and then to see that all was well, and his wife was helping the chef.

"What now, sir?"

"Douglas, Knell. Don't forget we've an appointment at nine with Monique Dol."

It was half-past eight when they got back to Douglas. It was still fully daylight. Littlejohn lit his pipe as they walked along the promenade. It was early in the holiday season, which hadn't yet got in full swing, and now it was all like a dress rehearsal for the busy weeks to come. All the cinemas, dance-halls and other entertainments were open. There was a throb of drums on the air and you could hear the shuffling and jigging of happy dancers through the open doors of the *Palace*.

People were still sitting in flannels and light dresses on the steps of boarding-houses and the seats of the promenade. His hands in his pockets and his pipe in his mouth, Littlejohn crossed with Knell to the *Carlton*.

There were now lights on in all the downstairs rooms and bars, and the dining-room was full. A small string band was playing softly in one of the lounges. The leader was the brother-in-law of the managing director whose wife had told him to find him a job. Otherwise, he'd have had the sack long ago and been replaced by a saxophonist and a double-bass slapper.

As the policemen entered by the revolving doors, kept in motion by a small boy with a dirty neck and wearing a pillbox hat, the hall-porter nodded to him and gave him a questioning look. He was the night man who hadn't seen the Superintendent before, but he recognised him from the photographs in the newspapers and the descriptions given below stairs. Also, he knew Knell, who'd run him in once for being drunk in charge. Littlejohn's arrival was a nuisance to him. Quite inopportune. He was busy bustling round a mob of guests who were leaving and another crowd of film people who'd decided to stay and had made him responsible for their bags. He'd his tips to collect.

People in evening dress were milling about. The co-stars were out in their full war-paint now that the show was on again. Model gowns, low-cut, showing as much of their bosoms as they dared. One of them was so exposed that the other women there, in a frenzy of jealousy, declared it was disgusting. Jewellery, mink coats—although the temperature was in the seventies—long cigars, expensive perfumes... The new overture to the film that almost hadn't come off. Jean Bizot entered dramatically and caused a general stir. He wasn't in the case, and hence to Littlejohn was a nonentity.

The night porter hung up the phone and hurried to Littlejohn. As he did so, he turned right and left all the way, greeting one and another just to remind them he was there and ready. To be sure of no other sideshows, he'd sent most of the rest of his staff off on trivial errands out of the way.

"I've just had a word with the manager, sir. He lives in a villa at Baldrine..."

Strange, with so many beds about, the manager had to run off to the country to sleep! He also had his own hens there and ate their eggs and wrung their necks, rather than suffer the products of his own *cordon bleu* chef.

"He says you're to have all you want and be given every facility."

Good of him!

"We have an appointment at nine with Miss Dol. Will you kindly let her know we're here?"

"Yes, sir. The late Mr. Vale's room's still locked. Just as Mr. Vale left it. Police instructions. Good evening, sir."

He greeted the disappointed comedian, who was passing with a lawyer and ignored him.

"Yes. I've got the key."

"Anything I can do, sir? I'm busy, but at your service."

"Please let Miss Dol have my message. Then we won't trouble you further."

They waited for him to return.

The groups hanging about in evening clothes had dined and now didn't know what to do with themselves. This wasn't London, Paris or Monte Carlo. No cabarets, nightclubs, or midnight bars. No night life at all. The dance-halls were out of the question, and to go to the cinemas and see rivals performing was no fun. They began to adjourn to the bars to drink off their boredom. In one corner of the smoke-room, a group of men were beginning to play poker.

An old gentleman with white hair, dressed in a blue lounge suit and soft collar, was asleep in an armchair with his mouth open. He looked like some Rip Van Winkle left behind from a previous existence. The honeymoon couple were fascinated by the film-stars and hung on their every word and gesture.

"She'll see you now, sir."

The porter took them up to the second floor and they entered by a door which led direct into the small salon which adjoined the bedroom.

"Good evening, Superintendent."

Monique Dol greeted Littlejohn like an old friend and he introduced Knell to her. She was dressed in an expensive white velvet evening gown with as much of the famous bosom showing as was allowed. She wore little jewellery, except expensive diamond ear-clips and a bracelet to match. They looked like presents from *mon oncle*. There was the usual scent of *Damnation* mildly on the air.

"Be seated, please."

Mauron had taught her good manners and grace of ways. She seemed genuinely glad to see them.

"May I offer you a drink?"

"No, thank you, Miss Dol. We don't wish to detain you..."

"I am visiting friends in Douglas and must be there before ten. The Governor will be present and I must be punctual, you see."

She spoke good English, with an attractive French accent.

"You wished to ask me some questions?"

"Yes, if you please. I'm very sorry about the upset of yet another death, this time in the flat at Aix. Do you feel able to answer one or two enquiries?"

"Of course."

She was sitting in a large antique wing chair, perfectly naturally and calmly. Her short hair was neatly and plainly dressed by an expensive expert and her hands, with their thin fingers, were controlled.

"Why did Mr. Armstrong come to visit you in Aix, after trying unsuccessfully to telephone you in Douglas after Vale's death? I know he found you'd left, but why was he there?"

"I think he was worried because I'd left the Isle of Man and held-up the filming. He was concerned with the finance, you know."

Littlejohn looked her straight in the eyes. She sometimes took the role of a defiant, incorrigible gamin in films, but now there was nothing of defiance there. Littlejohn thought he detected anxiety, almost fear. But you couldn't tell. She was an actress, after all.

"When I was in Cannes, Miss Dol, I had a long talk with Monsieur Mauron. He told me he had advised you to tell the truth to the police. W. J. Armstrong had no reason to fly all the way to the Mediterranean to discuss finance with you. He was anxious about something else. Have you any idea what it was?"

"I never saw him whilst he was there. I'd left before he arrived in Aix, as you know, Superintendent."

There was a pause of complete silence. Outside, in the sidestreet, someone began to play a Spanish air on a guitar.

"If you don't know, then, or cannot even make a guess, I'll ask you another question, Miss Dol. When you made your way to Mr. Vale's room and found him dead there, did you meet anyone or see anyone whose identity you guessed?"

"I said when you asked me before, Superintendent, that I thought someone entered the lift and went down."

"And you guessed who it was? It was Armstrong, wasn't it?"

"I didn't see him plainly. The corridor was not very well lighted."

"Miss Dol. You and the intruder were on the same corridor long enough for him to recognise *you*. Did you not recognise *him*? And *did* he go down the lift? Or did he take the staircase or pass through one of the doors which leads to the servants' quarters and down to the back entrance?"

"Monsieur Mauron has told you this?"

"It was, wasn't it, the problem you took to him in Cannes? Should you tell the police about W. J. Armstrong or shouldn't you? Monsieur Mauron advised you not to do so for the time being."

"That is right. As Paul has already told you, there is no point in my denying it."

She passed her tongue across her lips and her cheeks flushed.

"I didn't intend to obstruct the police. Please believe me. I was terrified and bewildered. I thought Mr. Armstrong had killed Hal because of their quarrel about me..."

"They quarrelled?"

"Mr. Armstrong was very fond of me and Hal was jealous. But their quarrel had been earlier in London about finance. Mr. Armstrong was, he said, happy to deal with financing a film in which I appeared, but he objected to Hal being in it. Paul intervened and finally Mr. Armstrong had to agree. But he hardly spoke to Hal again after it."

"Why did Monsieur Mauron suggest you kept quiet?"

She was losing her composure now.

"I am very upset. Do you mind if I have a drink, Superintendent? There is a bottle of champagne in my bedroom..."

Knell sought it out, opened it clumsily, spraying himself with wine in the effort, and finally poured out a glass for her. She drank it eagerly and held it out for a re-fill.

"Won't you two gentlemen drink, too?"

They thanked her and declined.

"I know you're in a hurry, Miss Dol. I will, therefore, tell you my own view of what happened and you can let me know if it agrees with the details you ought to be telling me..."

"Please. It will be much easier. I am very upset."

She lit a cigarette from a box on the table with nervous fingers. Then she offered them one each, which they accepted.

"First of all, I assure you I'm not trying to trick you, Miss Dol. So I'll be candid with you. Monsieur Mauron has told me nothing of what he advised you, except to speak the truth. You recognised Armstrong as he left Vale's room. When you saw Armstrong and then found Vale dead, you thought Armstrong was the murderer. He was Mauron's agent and you fled to Mauron in panic for advice. Am I right?"

"Yes..."

They could hardly hear the word.

"Monsieur Mauron advised you not to mention the matter. Perhaps he said Armstrong was not the murderer. Why should he be? He was a civilised man, capable of dealing with Vale in better ways than killing him. Even if Armstrong thought of murdering Vale to clear him out of the way as a rival for your love, he would know that it would do no good. That would not win you. Am I right?"

"You say Paul has not told you of our conversation. Strange. Your guess is correct."

"In other words, Armstrong found himself in the same position as you. He saw someone when he was on his way to Vale's room. Someone he thought he knew, but wasn't sure about. Perhaps, like you, he found the corridor too dark. However, I think he followed you to ask if you had seen Vale's murderer, too."

"I had not thought of it that way. I thought he went to Cannes to see Paul about it, found him absent, and decided to stay the night at Aix, in the flat, as he sometimes did."

"But Armstrong had a house near Cannes and could have stayed there. I think he was either seeking you to ask if you, too, had seen the intruder. Or else, thinking you had seen the intruder, who knew you had, hoping to protect you from him. However, the unknown one seems to have followed Armstrong to kill him, because he thought W. J. A. saw and recognised him outside Hal Vale's room after he'd killed him. Now, who was the unknown man?"

"I don't know. I swear I don't. I was almost too late to see Mr. Armstrong. The stranger had left before I appeared."

"I see. Then, I won't trouble you further on that matter. Just one more point. I believe Hal Vale was going to start a film company to deal with your productions?"

"That is right. After the trouble with Mr. Armstrong, Hal promised he would provide the finance himself."

"You were to be married after his divorce became absolute?"

"Yes."

"Forgive me, but I heard that you were rather long in deciding about it, Miss Dol."

She was now quite calm again and the question didn't perturb her.

"Yes. We quarrelled about the matter of finance. I said I would not have the upsets caused by Hal and Mr. Armstrong about money. I wished Hal to finance my films if I married him. He agreed and we were friends again and arranged about the marriage."

Just like that! No lovers' quarrels. Just a business deal as far as Monique Dol was concerned, and cash on the nail! Looking at her, Littlejohn thought how charming she was, superficially and for the public eye, yet utterly self-seeking and hard as nails beneath the veneer.

"Mr. Vale had the money?"

"He said he had. He had considerable funds with Paul, in his bank, he told me."

"I see. I think that will be all for the present, Miss Dol. Thank you for giving us some of your time. I hope this trouble will soon be over for you."

"So do I. Thank you for your kindness, Superintendent. I shall not forget it. Good-bye..."

They left her with a handshake and found themselves at the lift again.

Littlejohn looked Knell in the face. He hadn't had an evening off since Vale's arrival. It had all been bed and work for him and he was tired out.

"Go home now, old chap, and take a good night's rest. And thank you for everything..."

Knell could hardly speak for emotion at the thought that his work was approved. Littlejohn saw him off to the police car and was surprised as he stood on the steps to find that daylight was still about. The quiet of the Manx evening was drawing on, the tide was in, and standing off in Douglas Bay, was a lighted ship bringing Manx-Americans back for a visit, and a choir was singing *Ellan Vannin* to welcome them home.

8

BACK STAIRS

Littlejohn had questioned none of the staff about events around the time of Vale's death. He had left it all to Knell. Nor had he inspected the back-stairs of the *Carlton*, those parts where the life-blood of eating, sleeping and entertainment is generated to keep going the superficial façade of the hotel. In his questions to Monique Dol about the back-stairs, the side door, the secret passages which lay behind the very walls of the luxurious corridors, he had merely imagined them on the basis of past experience of such places.

There was a mahogany door, just past the main stairs and lifts, which nobody seemed to use. Littlejohn turned the knob and opened it. It led to the staff staircase which twisted upwards from a broad corridor. Littlejohn entered and closed the door behind him. The last he saw of the reception hall was the night porter eyeing him forbiddingly, but too busy taking instructions for the following morning to interfere.

A solitary light in a cheap shade hung from a brass bracket on the wall. The stairs climbed to the left; to the right, another door which the Superintendent pushed open. The world of the kitchens, all white tiles, stainless steel, polished aluminium and brass. Men in chef's uniforms and caps, women in white coats, porters in shirt sleeves and white aprons. At the far end in an alcove, a battery of sinks at which women with rolled-up sleeves were washing-up. Dinner was in progress and the whole place was alive with energy. Waiters running in and out, cooks carving joints and dismembering birds, now and then quarrels breaking-out. Littlejohn stepped back into the passage.

From where he was standing the vast underworld of the hotel opened up like secret, invisible arteries, veins and organs which kept the visible parts alive and comfortable. He mounted the staircase, cheaply carpeted, to the first floor. A landing, with doors open leading from it and revealing small sub-kitchens with morning tea-trays standing ready, and another room with a table and chairs where the staff apparently ate their meals or took their rest. There was nobody about, except a solitary woman pressing a pair of trousers with an electric iron and too immersed in the task to notice him.

Another door gave on to the first floor of the hotel. The sudden change of atmosphere from the almost shabby to the opulent came as quite a shock.

Behind the door, a fuse-box, which Littlejohn opened. Inside, amid the dust, the fuses were labelled and among them he could distinguish a recently cleaned one ticketed *Electric Razors*. Knell's men had been thoroughly over the lot without any useful results.

He resumed his tour upwards among the complicated stairs, passages, multiple doors of the personnel quarters. There was a faint, queasy odour of stale food over it all, hot and unventilated. Another landing and an entrance to the main second-floor corridor of the hotel. Opposite the door was that of the sitting-room of Monique Dol's suite. In a room behind, two chambermaids, a man and a kitchen-maid were eating supper, their elbows on the table, a bit dishevelled, their jaws moving with food and conversation. The man, dressed as a *valet de chambre*, raised his fatigued eyes and watched Littlejohn as he went out and then back again.

Littlejohn turned and disturbed the gathering. They were disposing of tea and bread-and-butter, and the man was smoking a cigarette at the same time. They resented the intrusion, especially the women, who were enjoying the company of the good-looking manservant.

"Sorry to disturb you, but were any of you on duty at the time Mr. Vale died?"

They all looked bored as though they were tired of the whole subject. The women turned their eyes first to Littlejohn and then to the valet, a youngish man with a crop of red hair, entreating him to be their spokesman.

"Yes; I think we were all on duty, but none of us saw a thing. We've talked it over and some of your chaps have questioned us a lot about it. You *are* from the police, aren't you?"

"Yes, I am. In the course of talking it over among yourselves, has the point been raised about somebody entering the hotel by the back door and prowling about the stairs and rooms of these rear quarters?"

"No. You see, about that time, all the teas were finished, and the staff would be in their rooms tidying themselves up for the evening. The maids and us men were all expected to be handy soon after for turning-down beds and making ourselves generally useful for those who were changing for dinner or going out."

"That would be around six to half-past?"

"Yes."

"But isn't that the time guests usually ring for service?"

"Yes. Sam, the valet on floor one, was on duty, of course. He was attending to Mr. Vale about that time. He found the body, you know. And then, Madge was on, too. She was looking after Miss Dol. The rest must have been elsewhere, because nobody mentioned finding strangers in the back parts."

The man crushed out his cigarette in his saucer and began to sharpen a match with his penknife to pick his teeth with.

"You might enquire, will you, among your colleagues if anybody suspicious was seen or heard?"

"I will, with pleasure, but I'm sure there wasn't. We'd have heard about it. Wouldn't we?"

He cast the question at the women, who backed him up with nods and affirmative noises and gave him glances of admiration for handling the matter so well.

Littlejohn returned to the ground floor and opened the outer door, which was barred and held secure by a large spring lock. He found himself in the street at the back of the hotel. A few yards away, on his left, another door, the luggage department. And again, on his right, the goods entrance to the kitchens. All the doors had been closed and fastened for the night. The luggage doorway was occupied by a couple locked in a close embrace. Over the shoulder of the man, who wore a white coat and looked like a bar waiter, the single visible eye of the girl, a blonde with an elaborate hair-do, was wide open, fixed on Littlejohn, like a glass one.

There was still a little reluctant daylight remaining. Littlejohn looked at his wrist-watch. 10.5. He left the loving couple, still immobile in their ecstasy, to their own devices and strolled round the maze of side-streets in the rear of the *Carlton*. Here both hotel and surroundings were shabby. The *Carlton* was spick and span at the front but needed a fresh coat of paint behind. The street, too, on which the back doors opened, was littered with rubbish and haunted by stray cats. Refuse, old paper, crusts of bread, straw covers from wine bottles, bins of stale food waiting for the pig-keepers to come and collect them. It all gave the impression of being cast out in haste by employees in too big a hurry to care where it fell.

Lights were now beginning to show in rooms of the second-rate hotels, pubs and tenement houses which rose all around this back street, gaunt, seedy, wearing a look of struggle, defeat, and waiting for the worst.

At the corner of the street, a shop, still illuminated, the window empty but tidy, and a card hanging on a hook held by a sucker on the pane.

Madame Alcardi, Palmist.
Horoscopes. Tarot Readings.
Patronised by Royalty.

Littlejohn entered the shop. The fittings had been cleared to make a fair-sized room, cheaply carpeted, stuffy. A table with a chair on each side and covered with a cloth printed with cabalistic figures. A physiognomy model-head on a stand in one corner; on the walls, framed signs of the zodiac and cards illustrated with shocking scenes, perhaps torn from Fox's *Booke of Martyrs*. A man hanging from a gallows, a woman being placed in a barrel full of spikes... A curtained doorway leading to the rear quarters faced the Superintendent as he entered.

A woman emerged, fat, flop-breasted, decked out in gold chains, bangles, rings and a pair of cheap pendulous earrings. She jingled as she walked. Her hair was bound in a soiled red kerchief. The smell of gin entered with her. She glanced warily at Littlejohn with her crafty, filmed eyes. She was half-washed.

"Yes?"

"Madame Alcardi?"

"No. Madame Alcardi died. I bought the business. I'm Madame Emmeline. You from the police?"

Perhaps she really had second-sight!

"Yes. I'm investigating the death of Hal Vale."

She clutched the goitre of her throat.

"Ah!"

At the mention of death, she was in the habit of almost automatically passing into a trance. She might even have had a shot at naming the murderer if she hadn't suddenly remembered Littlejohn was from the police.

"I know nothing about it."

"I didn't say you did. Does the window of the room behind overlook the *Carlton*?"

She sighed with relief. She thought Littlejohn might be one of the squad who came regularly, pretending to be holidaymakers or telling some lame tale, and then ran her in for telling fortunes.

"Yes, but I never saw Hal Vale there."

"Are you here all day?"

"Yes. Night, too. I live above."

"Were you here on the day Vale died? Say between five and six-thirty in the evening?"

"I never stir out..."

She looked it.

"... except to get a bit of food and the milk. My feet swell, you see, when I walk more than a yard or two."

"Were you looking through the window at that time?"

"I might have been. I can't remember, so long since, what I did and what I didn't."

"Are you sure?"

"Of course I am. I've something better to do than peep round the curtains watching the ins and outs of the back door of the *Carlton*. Although I could tell you a thing or two about what goes on there sometimes."

"I'm sure you could. Has it been busier there since the film company arrived?"

"No more than usual. They don't use the back doors. They want the limelight, that lot do. Their vans come and go with electrical stuff, properties, scenery and the like. No wonder prices are high at the movies, the amount of waste that goes on. You stopping there, too?"

"No."

"I remember now. The papers said you was at Grenaby. With the Venerable Archdeacon. Nice man, Mr. Kinrade..."

"I agree. You said the vans come and go. Do they unload stuff at the back, then?"

"Yes. Films and cameras and talkie apparatus, it looked like."

"Any unloaded at the time Hal Vale was killed?"

"I can't say. I told you, it's no use asking me."

"Weren't you looking out when Hal Vale's body was brought out by the luggage exit and put in the mortuary-van?"

"Yes. I saw the van come and wait. I recognised it and I wanted to see what it was doin' there. I saw them bringin' out the body. I knew somethin' 'orrible was going to happen. I felt it all the day."

"Did you see Miss Dol leave by the back door earlier, then? I suppose you'd recognise Miss Dol if you saw her?"

"Yes, I did."

"Why didn't you say so before?"

"You never asked me..."

Which was to be expected. In her profession she was in the habit of slowly ladling out the facts or fiction of her so-called 'readings', the fruits of her second-sight. It was no use delivering it in spate; it had to be revealed gradually and in mental labour. Otherwise clients would think she wasn't giving them their money's worth.

"She slowly opened the door, peeped out, saw that nobody was about, and then ran. Or tried to run. Her heels was too high for runnin'... She was carryin' a blouse-case sort of affair. From the front I saw her stop a car passin' down Broadway and ask for a lift..."

"Did the driver seem to know her?"

"No. They had a sort of conversation first and then he seemed to tell her to get in."

"Did you recognise him?"

"No."

"The car?"

"'No. They was too far away.'"

"Now think carefully, Madame Emmeline. Did anyone enter by a back door just before Monique Dol came out?"

Madame Emmeline paused, as though searching her memory.

"There's always somebody comin' and goin' there. Which door?"

"The middle one. The staff entrance."

"As I said there's a lot of going in and out."

"Do you know all the personnel at the *Carlton* from seeing them at the back door?"

"Yes, mostly. They're always changin', but I get to know them."

"Any strangers between say, five and half-past six the day Mr. Vale died?"

Madame Emmeline showed signs of becoming very restive.

"Look. 'ow much longer's this goin' to last? I'm in business and it might be keepin' customers away. If they peep through the curtains and see..."

"They can't see a thing. If you're suggesting you want paying for your time, I'll pay your fee. But only if you have something useful to tell me. The reason I've been here so long is your diffidence in giving me any help. Now, have you anything to tell me?"

"Yes."

He handed her five shillings. She looked at it hard and might have been about to spit on the coins for good luck.

"This is the lowest fee I accept, and only then from people who can't afford more."

"Well, you can take it, then, Madame, that *I* can't afford more. What have you to tell me?"

She gulped.

"At about quarter to six that night, I saw a man called Armstrong go in at the servants' door of the *Carlton*. That's all. He knocked hard and when one of the kitchen hands opened it, he went in. The man didn't like it and was for stopping him. Armstrong gave him some money and he let him in."

"How do you know it was Armstrong? He's only a holiday-maker here and he's hardly the type who comes to you for his fortune to be told."

"Excuse me! I don't tell fortunes, so don't you be tryin' to catch me out. I know Armstrong because I've seen his picture in the paper."

"Do you remember everybody whose pictures are in the paper, then?"

"No. But I take out newspaper cuttings durin' the season, of all accounts of the people I can."

Of course! It was part of her trade to collect information and then, if any interested party came for a reading, she'd trot it out as if she'd learned it by her powers of precognition.

"Do you happen to have the picture?"

"Yes. But five bob isn't much for..."

"Get it, please."

She rummaged in a drawer in a kind of sideboard along one wall and produced a large book labelled *Christmas Cards*. It was an old sample book from which the cards had been torn and cuttings stuck in their places. After a lot of page-turning and heavy breathing, she at last found what she wanted.

"There!"

It was quite a good likeness in its way, and showed W. J. Armstrong arriving at Ronaldsway from a 'plane.

W. J. Armstrong, the London banker, who represents the syndicate financing the film "Women Who Wait", soon to be shot on the Isle of Man.

"Thank you. I'd like to take this picture. You're quite sure he was the man you saw enter the back door?"

"Of course I am. I saw him as plain as the nose on your face. It was him. He's the sort you don't forget, you see. Tall, important, masterful, like. I want that picture, though."

He tore it out, and folded and put the page in his pocket. Then he handed her another five shillings.

"It's no use to you. He's dead."

"I knew he wouldn't last long as soon as I clapped my eyes on him. I'd a feeling..."

"Has Inspector Knell been here making enquiries?"

The woman's face turned positively sour.

"Well..."

"Yes, he has, hasn't he? Did you tell him about Armstrong?"

"No. Why should I? He's no friend of mine."

"It was your duty."

"That's what he said when he was a bobby on the beat and ran me in for fortune-tellin', as he called it. I asked him to give me another chance. He said it was his duty, and they fined me two pounds... As I said, he's no friend of mine, so why should I?"

Littlejohn left her to her brooding and her bottle and went into the open air again. It seemed full of ozone after the fug in the shop.

At the corner facing the rear of the *Carlton*, a small boarding-house, *Cranbrook Hotel. Running water in all Rooms*. A flight of stone steps leading up to the door. The fanlight was illuminated by a bulb in a bead shade. The place looked empty. A man in his shirt sleeves, leaning against the doorpost looking up and down the street and smoking the last of a cigarette.

"Nice evening."

"Yes. You the detective from across?"

"Yes. You the owner?"

He looked like a retired sergeant-major gone to seed. All that was left of his former glory was a heavy grey moustache waxed into points, somewhat askew.

"Yes and no. Missus runs the place. I'm odd job man."

He said it in a defeated, resigned way, pushed another battered cigarette in the corner of his mouth, and lit it from the stub of the other.

"What can I do for you?"

The street was deserted except for a large grey tomcat on the prowl. The man was obviously bored and out for a long talk if he could get it.

"You've got a good view of the *Carlton* back-door from here."

"Yes. We see all the comin' and goin's, as you might say. When it's sunny, you'll find me here most of the day; when it's rainin', I squint through the side window. Don't miss much. You see, I'm supposed to be on the lookout for stragglers among the visitors who might not have booked digs and are on the hunt for some. Then I suggest they come 'ere."

He smiled and passed his hand across his loose mouth as though he were thirsty.

"Do you remember the evening Hal Vale died?"

"Yes. I saw all the comin's and goin's..."

The comin's and goin's seemed to be the main part of the tout's experience.

"Anything useful for the police?"

"Can't say there was. You'll know all about they brought the body out of the back-door to the ambulance, and all the official comin's and goin's, like."

"Yes."

"Well, there's nothin' much more. It's mostly the employees and tradesmen use the back, you see. Although I must say I got a good look at Monica Dol there the night Vale died. I saw her come out that way. Then, soon after, I see it in the papers that she'd bolted to France."

"Yes. We know about that."

The sergeant-major's moustache trembled and he drew himself up to his full height. It made him stagger a bit, for he wasn't used to doing it. He then thrust his face into Littlejohn's.

"Well, here's somethin' you don't know..."

He paused for dramatic effect and puffed whisky over Littlejohn.

"At about the time they said Hal Vale died, I saw a man come out by the back door of the *Carlton*, look round to see if anybody was watchin', and then clear off hell-for-leather. He didn't see me. I was indoors at the window. Did you know *that*?"

"No."

Littlejohn took out the newspaper cutting bearing Armstrong's photograph. They put their heads together over it under the light in the hall.

"Was that the man?"

The sergeant-major scrutinised it carefully. He even turned it upside down, as if that could do any good. But he was just showing he was doing the job properly.

"Not a bit like 'im. This chap was a toff, judgin' from the way he was dressed. Tallish, dark suit, and although it was 'ellish hot, he'd a summer overcoat on with the collar turned-up. He was too far away for me to see his face, and he was wearin' sunglasses and a hat turned down all round."

"How tall?"

"About as tall as me, I'd say."

About five feet ten, or perhaps a little more, according to how tall the man fancied himself. Age and drink had reduced him from his former height to a bent and shambling caricature of what he'd once been in the Guards.

"Is that all you can tell me about him?"

"Yes. As I said before, he was too far away for me to see what he looked like."

"Did he have a car waiting for him? Did you see how he got away?"

"As far as I could see, he went off on foot. Made his way to Derby Road and along there. I couldn't see what he did after that."

"Well, thanks very much. You've been a great help."

"Pleasure, I'm sure."

What next? At present they'd got a lot of unidentified, shadowy figures which required the details painting-in. So far, they'd traced W. J. Armstrong to the back door of the *Carlton*. He'd been a man who avoided crowds and publicity and must have had a paid hand in the rear of the hotel to admit him when he wanted to call there. And the only reason for such calls was probably Monique Dol. Armstrong had been on his way to see Vale about her, as likely as not, when he found Vale dead in his bath. W. J. A. had perhaps remembered the man he'd met on the corridor, and, putting two and two together, decided he was the killer. Whether or not Armstrong had finally made up his mind who the intruder was would probably never be known. But the intruder had seen W. J. A., and, after that, thought him best out of the way. He'd run him down in Aix-en-Provence... The man in the sunglasses, turned-down hat, and coat with the collar up.

The man in the sun-glasses had got as far as Derby Road and then vanished from sight of the watching ex-sergeant major.

Littlejohn slowly returned to the *Carlton*, puffing his pipe gently. It was a pleasant night, calm and warm, and the promenade was illuminated and full of happy revellers.

He didn't know whether or not a room had been reserved for him at the *Carlton*. He'd forgotten to ask them. If they hadn't made a reservation... well the key of Hal Vale's old suite was in his pocket. That would do! Reserved for the police.

Knell hadn't failed him, however. The porter led him up to a first-class room on the front. They'd even unpacked his bag and put his things away. His pyjamas were laid-out on the turned-down bed and, as the hall-porter was quick to point out, there was a bottle of whisky and a syphon on his bedside table with the compliments of the management.

Littlejohn picked up the room telephone and asked for the police station.

"Who is it?"

"Sergeant Skillicorn speaking."

"Littlejohn."

"Gooood evenin', sir. What can I do for you?"

He told Skillicorn that he knew Knell was off duty. He was not to be disturbed. Would the police, however, visit every house, hotel, boarding house and pub in Derby Road, and ask if anyone had seen a man answering to the description, given by the tout, of the man in sun-glasses who left the *Carlton* at the time of Vale's death?

If he'd been seen, where did he go? Enter a taxi? Turn the corner? Vanish in the distance? If possible, he's to be traced to his ultimate destination.

"I realise this is a big job, Skillicorn, but it's vital..."

"It'll be a pleasure to do it for you, sir. We'll have all the men we can spare out in Derby Road around breakfast-time before the visitors go out. There's always someborry looking out of the window, taking a skeet at what's going on. I'd be surprised if we didn't find one, at least, who'd seen him and knew what happened to him."

"I hope so. Thanks very much, Skillicorn."

Next morning at 8.45, just as Littlejohn was ready to go down for breakfast, his telephone rang. It was Knell.

"Good morning, sir. Nice morning..."

You could almost see him rubbing his hands with pleasure.

"We got the information about the man in Derby Road, sir."

"You did! Already?"

"No trouble, sir. The second house our men visited. A man who'd been looking out of the window as he waited for his tea, saw this queer chap, in sun-glasses, and wondered what he wanted with a coat and collar turned-up with the sun blazing down and the thermometer at over seventy. He watched him along the road. Said he looked a bit jumpy and kept glancing behind him. He walked almost to the end of Derby Road and then got in a taxi waiting for him."

"I congratulate you all, Knell. This is splendid."

"There's more, sir. We rang up the taxi proprietors. Two of them called Cregeen and Kneale remembered the fellah. But they can't improve on the description. The man rang up Kneale and told him to wait for him at a certain number in Derby Road at 6.15 to take him to the airport. Kneale says he thinks he caught the 7.05 'plane to London. I'm sorry they couldn't better the description. Cregeen was on the cab-rank at the airport and the man picked him up at 5.30, or about that, and asked him to get him to Douglas quickly. He dropped him at the Broadway end of Derby Road."

"You've done splendidly..."

The Manx police were certainly on their toes!

"We telephoned the airport and described him. They confirmed that he'd joined the London 'plane at 7.05. We asked his name. They said it was Smith."

Not so good!

As he hung up the instrument it rang again.

"A call from the Dublin police, sir. The Douglas police have had it put through."

Clara Tebbs again! They'd got her at Athlone and the Irish police were finding her an embarrassment. What had she done wrong? How could they arrest and hold her if there was no case? She'd told quite a good story. When on her excursion, she'd decided to stay in Eire and left the party. As simple as that. She was prepared to face the English police or anybody else for that matter. She wouldn't run away, she said.

Littlejohn almost told them he'd tell Scotland Yard to send a man over, and then he changed his mind.

"I'll come myself on the morning 'plane..."

Hal Vale had been on the 'plane from Dublin to the Isle of Man, the first time he'd met him. What had he been doing in Dublin?

9
MAN IN DARK GLASSES

On the short 'plane journey to Dublin, Littlejohn, enjoying a rare quietness, brooded on the case.

The motive for Hal Vale's murder was difficult to sort out. Could it have been his forthcoming marriage with Monique Dol? That would involve W. J. Armstrong. If so, how was the death of Armstrong tied-up with that of Vale?

Or, could it have been that Vale's marriage in some way threatened the livelihood, the social standing, the very existence of someone in his entourage? His recent experience had showed Littlejohn a flock of hangers-on who were doing very well out of Vale. Easy living, lavish spending, all the luxuries and privileges of following a film-star round the world.

Mauron, Armstrong, McLeary, Firmin, even Monique Dol herself were members he'd already interviewed. Then there were Hal Vale's past wives, and their husbands, whom the Superintendent hadn't yet met, but might need to find at any time.

Before he could answer any of his own questions, they were in Dublin, a police-car met him at the airport, and he was taken to the police station to interview Clara Tebbs.

The Tebbs affair was almost like a comic opera which kept

superimposing itself on the complicated tragedy of Hal Vale!

Clara faced Littlejohn proudly. She was now Clara Muldoon! She was accompanied by her husband, too, an ex-New York policeman, if you please, who'd come home to Ireland to end his days with his pension.

"I didn't want pestering by my creditors..."

Clara Tebbs had been on the verge of bankruptcy. Writs, lawyers and debt-collectors always on the doorstep of her small grocer's shop. After walking round Dublin on the day of her disappearance, she'd sat on the wall of Trinity College to ease her feet, indulged in conversation with a large man, who had gone so far as to remove his boots to ease his own. This trivial bond in common had grown, they had had tea together, and had stayed the night in Dublin. Separate hotels! That was emphasised. And he had then taken her to Athlone, the place where he was born. Clara Tebbs had told him the story of her life and they had forgotten the departed excursionists from which Clara had separated herself to their discomfiture, and her creditors in London, had married, and had let the rest of the world go by.

As far as Littlejohn was concerned, the case of Clara Tebbs was closed. What her creditors and existing distant relatives did was no concern of his. Ex-patrolman F-X. Muldoon seemed robust enough to look after them all on his wife's behalf.

Superintendent Higgins of the Irish police took Littlejohn to lunch. It was a good lunch and lasted two hours. In the course of that time, Mr. Higgins's subordinates set about obtaining all the information Littlejohn had asked for about Hal Vale.

Hal Vale had spent two days in Dublin before he left for the Isle of Man and his almost immediate death there. He had stayed at the Shelbourne Hotel. So had Mrs. Marie Vale, his ex-wife. Like Clara Tebbs and F-X. Muldoon, separate rooms, of course! Firmin had also been there. They had visited during their stay, according to information from the hall-porter and telephonist, Messrs. O'Casey and Poole, Solicitors, of Fitzwilliam Place.

Messrs. O'Casey and Poole had long since died and a certain Mr. Collins was now running the firm. Their offices were in a fine old house with a magnificent Georgian frontage, ornamental ceilings, and splendid woodwork. Mr. Collins himself, a tall, dark, savage-looking man, proved more hospitable than he looked. He knew Higgins well and therefore was disposed to talk within the bounds of professional etiquette. Over glasses of well-matured Irish whiskey, he candidly disclosed that Vale, his divorced wife, and Firmin had been in Dublin to discuss alimony.

"The Doyle family have been clients of this firm for more than a century. They were landed people from Kildare and even when Marie married Vale, she would have no other lawyers but us for her affairs."

The windows were open and the street quiet. Beyond, the distant noises of the town. Outside it was sunny and the hot air entered the cool room in little gusts.

"Of course, I knew when she married a man with the reputation of Hal Vale that she was doing the wrong thing. Her first husband was a heavy drinker and lost preferment in the diplomatic service. He neglected Marie badly and dragged her to some queer places in the course of his career, but he wasn't an outsider like Vale. De Beer had, at least, some breeding..."

"I suppose, Mr. Collins, that you and Firmin dealt with Vale's will when he married Marie de Beer?"

"We did. Firmin was a man I didn't like at all. One of those slick commercial lawyers who'd turn his hand to anything for a sizeable fee. He, of course, had made and had the will signed before I came into the picture. It was a matter of trusts in Marie's favour that interested me. Trusts Firmin and Vale made in manoeuvring out of tax in England. To be brief, Vale's will left Marie as residuary legatee of an estate which Firmin said was worth over a hundred thousand pounds."

Mr. Collins thereupon took out a pipe, filled it with black tobacco, lit it, and emitted clouds of strong smoke.

"You'll take a cigar?"

He passed a box to Littlejohn and Higgins, who both lighted up. The room was soon in a fog which drifted here and there as the hot air from the window drove it about.

"And the divorce naturally deprived her of all the benefits under the will?"

"Yes. Vale had instructed Firmin to make a new will, passing on the residue of his estate to the French girl... Miss Dol... as soon as they married. The will would be signed immediately after the ceremony. It was a friendly arrangement between Vale and Marie. In spite of the divorce they were quite friendly. I do not understand these modern ways of regarding marriage."

"Meanwhile, the old one would operate until the decree became absolute in a week or so?"

"That is correct. Marie Vale will now, after all, inherit the residue of Vale's fortune after certain small legacies have been paid."

Mr. Collins seemed to grow more and more dishevelled as he smoked and discussed the case. His hair was ruffled and his face was flushed and savage.

"I disapprove of divorce, on principle, but professionally, I'm bound to serve my clients. Marie Vale has had a pretty bad deal with Vale since she married him. The man was a libertine, and his mean selfish ways were written large on his face. I'm not surprised he came to a bad end."

"Is she likely to marry again very soon?"

Mr. Collins reared his leonine head in anger.

"With her late husband not yet in his grave, that's a strange question to ask about a decent girl. The answer's certainly not."

But, it seemed, Mr. Collins didn't know everything.

The deputy hall-porter at the hotel, a fellow named Costello, was most informative when Littlejohn questioned him. He had a brother-in-law in the Dublin police and was very deferential to

Higgins with a view to preserving his brother-in-law's good name.

"Hal Vale, although a famous film star, wasn't my cup-o'-tea at all. Fond of the ladies and neglected his wife shocking!"

Costello didn't know, of course, that the meeting at the hotel was simply an unemotional one to arrange about alimony and divorce.

"We found Mrs. Vale a perfect lady all the time she was here. Mr. Firmin, the man who was with them, a lawyer, I was told, seemed to think the same as me. A lady. As a matter of fact, I wouldn't be surprised if he wasn't sweet on her himself."

"What makes you think that?"

"Well, Mr. Vale was out on his own most of the time they was here. He occupied a room on the floor above his wife, too. The late hours he got in! Long after his wife had gone to bed. Well, Mr. Firmin hardly left Mrs. Vale. If I hadn't known from the reception desk that Vale was her husband, I'd have thought Firmin was the lucky man. She seemed very fond of him, too, although decent, like, I'd have you know... They dined and went out together and they was happy and laughin' together whenever Vale wasn't around. That man looked as if he created misery and long faces wherever he went."

As Littlejohn knew, Hal Vale had parted from Marie and Firmin in Dublin and travelled alone to the Isle of Man. Higgins took him to the airport office off O'Connell Street and had the records turned up.

Vale's and Littlejohn's bookings were there on the same flight. Marie Vale had booked through to London and Nice; left the same day as Vale, only earlier. She had, according to Costello, who'd seen about a taxi for her and her luggage, received a cable from France which made her decide to leave Dublin as quickly as possible. That would be Mauron's invitation to the Mediterranean cruise.

Of Firmin's moves there was no trace at all.

Littlejohn remembered that Firmin had been in London at the time of Vale's death, according to his statement. That meant that he had left Eire before Vale. He'd surely have travelled there with Marie. Yet there was no trace of his name in the London flights. The Irish Superintendent thereupon spoke to the hall-porter at the Shelbourne Hotel again. Firmin had left for London on the morning 'plane next after Marie, according to his own story, and had said good-bye to Vale and Marie immediately after breakfast. There was no booking for Firmin on any London run. And he could not possibly have made the journey to London in time by sea.

Then an idea struck Littlejohn. He wrote out as full a description as he could of the man in dark glasses, from information given by the queer residents behind the *Carlton*, the lodger in Derby Road, and the taxi drivers. Superintendent Higgins questioned airport officials, none of whom remembered the strange man who seemed to be trying to conceal his identity.

Together the two policemen consulted flight schedules.

Littlejohn finally placed his finger on an afternoon flight, a special summer one for holiday purposes.

Dublin 17.05.

I.O.M. 17.40.

"I wonder if the stewardess of that 'plane remembers such a man?"

And he gave Higgins the date.

More records, more heads together. Miss Mary Baggot, of 27, Quarry Road, Glasnevin, had been serving on the 'plane in question at the stated time. Miss Baggott was off duty for the day.

A very pleasant car ride to Glasnevin brought them to Quarry Street, a short thoroughfare showing no signs of its namesake. The house was one of a terrace of Georgian-fronted dwellings looking a bit worse for wear and, when Higgins rang the bell, an elderly lady answered it and said she was Mary's mother and what might the gentlemen be wanting. When she heard they were from the police, she didn't seem much impressed, said she was a widow, and asked them indoors.

"Mary's out with her young man..."

She then gave them each a cup of tea, which seemed to have been ready and waiting for them, told them to make themselves comfortable, and went next door to telephone Mary to come home at once.

Mrs. Baggot was soon back, filled-up their cups, gave them each a piece of cake, and told them that it was Mary's birthday, that her boy-friend, who was a Customs officer also having his afternoon off, had taken her out for a meal. That they would be back in ten minutes. They arrived half an hour later.

Mary Baggot was a clean, rosy Irish beauty of the type whose pictures appear on advertisements for holidays in Eire, and proved to be very intelligent and observant.

"I remember the man you describe, sir. He was on the 'plane last and off first. His name on the check-list was Jones. He took a seat, never spoke and never stirred. He looked as if someone had done him wrong. He wore his sun-glasses all the time and kept his hat on all the way. A black slouch one. I can't improve upon your description. Except... yes... As he lifted his hand to adjust his glasses, I saw he'd a large signet ring with a stone in it on the left little finger."

The Customs officer, a tall, solemn young man, stood jealously by whilst all this was going on. Littlejohn felt that if he ever met him in the course of his travels, his bags and any contraband would have a rough passage.

The signet ring. Littlejohn remembered it when he'd interviewed Firmin. Things were looking a bit clearer at last.

Firmin and Marie Vale were, according to Costello, very fond of each other. Could it be that they were waiting for the divorce to get married? Firmin and Marie had been in each other's company quite a lot since her marriage to Vale. Perhaps, in Costello's terms, they'd got sweet.

But, it was far better for Marie to marry Firmin as Vale's widow, instead of his divorced wife. She would inherit his fortune. Firmin had made the will and knew it all. Unless Vale died before his marriage to Monique Dol, Marie would merely be left with a few thousands a year in alimony. If Vale died before the new will was executed, Firmin would get Marie and Vale's fortune as well.

"Could I telephone, please, Mrs. Baggot?"

Mrs. Baggot took him with her to the neighbour's. This caused some commotion, for, as soon as she introduced him as Superintendent Littlejohn to Mr. Connolly, the man next door, he turned pale and swept a lot of papers from his desk in what seemed eagerness to give Littlejohn plenty of room.

Littlejohn telephoned to Scotland Yard and asked that a man be assigned to keep Firmin in view. He might either be at Vale's funeral at Golder's Green, or at his flat, or in his office.

He then thanked Mr. Connolly, who seemed so relieved that he offered Littlejohn a drink of old Irish whiskey, which the Superintendent humorously disposed of, just to show there was no ill-feeling. And Mr. Connolly gave him a hearty handshake and told him if he could ever do anything for him, to let him know.

Back in Dublin there were more air schedules to consult. This time B.E.A. from the Isle of Man to London.

I.O.M. 7.05.

London 8.30.

Then, a telephone call to the Isle of Man airport, police office.

"Please ask if the stewardess on the 'plane for London leaving 7.05 on the evening Hal Vale died is available and ring me back at Dublin police headquarters."

Finally word came through. Miss Thompson, the stewardess in question, had arrived half-an-hour before on an incoming 'plane, was due out again the following morning, and would be staying the night on the Island. She was at the elbow of the telephoning policemen. She was soon at the other end of the 'phone.

"Hullo. Is that Miss Thompson?"

"Yes, sir."

"Do you remember the last 'plane to London, last Saturday, on which you were serving?"

"Yes. It was a special summer 'plane, running late for night connections with the Continent."

"Do you recollect a passenger, a man, who all the time wore sun-glasses and probably kept on his hat?"

"I certainly do. He was very rude. He never spoke, not even in answer to civil questions. He arrived very late at the airport and we'd had to call for him over the loud-speaker."

"Anything special about his behaviour?"

"His rudeness. And also a funny thing he did. Half way across, he locked himself in the lavatory, which he entered with his hat on. He took with him, also, a small suitcase, which he'd checked-in as hand luggage. I think it contained a suit into which he changed."

"Why?"

"He'd a coat on over his suit when he joined the 'plane. He kept it on all the time. I couldn't see any part of his suit except the bottoms of the trousers. When he came aboard, they were navy-blue pin-stripe. When he went off at London, they were black and looked like those of a dinner-suit. His collar was up and the coat buttoned, so I couldn't make out if he wore a dress shirt and black tie..."

"Thank you very much, Miss Thompson. I'm very grateful for your help."

"That's O.K., sir. A pleasure."

Littlejohn would have liked to stay and enjoy the delightful hospitality of the Dublin police a little longer. Things were warming up, however. He left by the last 'plane for London.

10
LONDON

It was ten o'clock when Littlejohn arrived in London. The first thing he did was telephone his wife and tell her he was back again.

"Sorry, Lettie, I won't be home till late."

"It's turned ten already."

"It may be in the small hours."

"I'll be waiting up for you with a cold meal..."

The nightclub known as *The Winking Light*, in Soho, was in full swing when Littlejohn called there at eleven o'clock. There wasn't a seat available, the place was hot and stuffy, and the manager was in a bad temper.

"My chef left me in the lurch just before we opened. I'm having to give a hand in the kitchen myself..."

He didn't look it. He was immaculately turned out. A little dark man with eyes like black shoe-buttons, who'd probably originated somewhere in the Middle East. He brightened up when he heard Littlejohn wanted information which didn't include questions about *The Winking Light*, which had a mixed reputation.

"Oh, yes. Mr. Firmins. Nice gentleman. Good client. Good sorts, eh?"

"Yes. He was here last Saturday, he tells me."

"I seemta remember. Yes. That's right. Pity about Mr. Hal Vales. Somebody brought the news about Mr. Vales bein' dead to Mr. Firmins while he was here that night."

"What time did Mr. Firmin arrive?"

"About ten."

"How do you know?"

The manager looked upset.

"Now, Mr. Littlejohns, I wouldn't tell you a lie. I know because the table was booked for nine, see? Oh, dear. I'd like to go now. No chef, you see."

He seemed worried about something and it wasn't the cooking.

"I won't keep you much longer. The table was booked for nine. Who was in the party?"

"It was a birthday party. A Mr. Fowlers and wife. And there was also Coopers and lady, and Mr. Firmins and his friend, Miss Marriotts..."

To Mr. Monides, they were all in the plural!

"They were all here at what time?"

"Nine-thirty. They's always late, you see. Mr. Firmins came about half-hour later. Said he'd been held-up in a taxi in a traffics jam. Which is quite true. Traffics jams in Soho enough to break your heart."

"You're sure?"

"Of course. You ask any of his friends. They'll tell you."

Littlejohn was sure Monides would change the time if Firmin asked him, provided all the rest would do the same. But now, he was strangely anxious to keep on the right side of the police. No awkward questions, no raids, no searchings... With his brother-in-law, Theodore, in the cellar hiding-out after a smash-and-grab that didn't come off, he couldn't run any risks. But, of course, Littlejohn didn't know about Theo.

"Always happy to oblige, Superintendents..."

It was midnight when Littlejohn and Cromwell reached Firmin's flat in Sloane Street. The Superintendent had picked up his friend the sergeant at Scotland Yard after reluctantly getting him from his bed in Shepherd Market.

"Sorry, old man, to turn-up at this hour and get you out of bed. I want you with me when I question a suspect in the Hal Vale case."

"Anywhere any time with you, sir."

It did him good to hear it after all the strange people and places of the past few days!

Firmin had just got in. He was in dinner clothes with a dressing-gown instead of a jacket and was drinking whisky and soda.

"Bit late, aren't you, Superintendent? I'm just going to bed. Have a nightcap with me?"

"No, thank you, sir."

"Some important development about Hal? I can't think you'd be here for anything else at this hour."

"I wish to ask you a few questions, sir. You need not answer them, Mr. Firmin, and I must warn you that anything you say may be taken down and used in evidence..."

"Look here, Littlejohn. What's all this? You're surely not proposing to arrest me for Hal's murder. That's ridiculous. What are you doing here at all?"

"The last time you and I talked together, sir, you told me that, as a lawyer, you were in duty bound to tell me the truth. Why didn't you?"

Firmin looked nasty. He must have been at the end of a thick night, for his face was lined and pale and his heavy eyelids were more swollen than ever.

"You calling me a liar?"

"You told me you were in London at the time of Hal Vale's death."

"So I was."

"You were not, sir. You were at the *Carlton*, Douglas, which you entered by the back door, wearing sun-glasses and a hat turned down to hide your face."

"Who told you all this rubbish?"

"You still deny it?"

"Of course I do."

"May we sit down and talk this over, sir?"

"Of course you can't sit down at this time of night, and we'll discuss the matter in the morning."

"I'm quite happy to remain standing. But unless you can give me some satisfactory explanation of your strange movements on Saturday last, I shall have to arrest you on suspicion of the murder of Hal Vale..."

Firmin's jaw dropped and he looked ready for violence.

"Why... You..."

"Please let me speak. It's no use sparring like this. You left Dublin last Saturday on the 'plane which reached the Isle of Man at 5.40. You went by taxi to Douglas and there you telephoned for another taxi to meet you at 6.15 in Derby Road. You'd cut yourself down to a very fine schedule, but with plenty of time to do as you wished. You entered by the back door of the *Carlton*, you went up to Hal Vale's room, you saw W. J. Armstrong on your way and dodged him, and you killed Vale in his bath..."

Firmin was so angry that he forgot he was holding a glass half-full and with a pugnacious gesture flung the contents over himself. He didn't seem to notice it.

"It's a lie! I was in London when all this was supposed to be going on. You can't find a victim, so you've picked on me. Well, I'm going to bed now and I'll be obliged if you'll both remove yourselves..."

"Not until you've heard all I have to say."

"You take the risk, then. I shall report this first thing tomorrow."

"You will do as you wish about it, sir. Meanwhile, you left the *Carlton* by the way you'd entered, got your taxi, caught the 7.5

plane to London, changed into evening clothes on the 'plane, and arrived at *The Winking Light* at 10.0—not 9.0, as you told me."

"Who gave you that nonsense?"

"Two taxi-drivers on the Isle of Man, a lodger in Derby Road, two air hostesses on the 'planes you used, two tenants of property behind the *Carlton* and overlooking the staff entrance at the back, and people at *The Winking Light*, who know the time you arrived. You travelled from Dublin under the name of Jones and from the Isle of Man as Smith. Very original!"

"Have you finished with your rigmarole? A lot of nonsense. I'll soon make mincemeat of that. But not at this hour of the morning. I'll deal with you later."

"You'll deal with me here and now, Mr. Firmin. Unless, as I said, you can offer a satisfactory explanation of your conduct, you will accompany me to Scotland Yard..."

"Answer me one thing, Littlejohn. Seeing you're so clever, why would I want to kill Hal Vale? He meant much more to me alive than dead, you know."

Firmin had cooled off. He was showing some interest now, the interest of a man confident of his position.

"I admit Vale was worth more to *you* alive than dead. But not to Marie Vale."

The shot landed home. Firmin lost his temper.

"Keep her out of this. She's had enough to go through without your making matters worse."

"In a few days' time, Mr. Firmin, Marie Vale's divorce becomes absolute. Vale then proposed to execute a new will in favour of his next wife. When they married, the benefits of his estate to the extent of over a hundred thousand pounds passed from Marie Vale to Monique Dol. You had five days in which to kill Hal Vale..."

"*I* had five days? You're mad. Why had I five days?"

"You are in love with Marie Vale and she feels the same about you. You planned to marry, with the benefit of the hundred thousand pounds, of course."

Firmin sat down and helped himself to another drink. Then he mopped his forehead.

"I've got to hand it to you, Littlejohn. You tell a good tale, but I tell you very calmly that you're dealing with a lawyer now and I'll make you pay for this dirty linen if it's the last thing I do."

"As regards the motive, we have also witnesses in Dublin who are aware of the mutual feelings of you and Marie Vale. Lawyer or not, you will have great difficulty in convincing a jury that you had nothing whatever to do with or gain from Hal Vale's death. Now, I ask you to consider what I've said, and if you have any explanation to give me, to give it at once."

"I didn't kill Hal Vale."

It was said so categorically, Littlejohn would almost have said so sincerely, that for a moment he was taken aback.

"If so, it's to your interest to explain your cloak-and-dagger behaviour at the time of the crime. You obviously know what it's all about, even if you didn't commit the murder, which I do not accept in view of your conduct. Have you anything to say?"

"Sit down. Have a drink? No? Then I'll have another."

He helped himself, guzzled it down, and paused to think, looking hard at his empty glass. In the flats, there wasn't a sound. Outside, the footsteps of some solitary late-bird echoed on the pavement.

"I'll make a bargain with you. I'll tell you all I know about Vale... or as much as you want to know, on condition that I'm not pestered any more by this crack-brained idea you've just been airing. It's all a pack of untruths, you're trying to catch me out, and I'm not biting, see?"

"I'm not making any such bargain with you, sir. This isn't a court of law and you're not the defending solicitor yet. But unless you tell me the truth now, I shall ask you to accompany me and I shall make a charge against you."

"Then, we'll call the whole thing off and I'll come with you and hear what the charge is about. You'll simply make a fool of yourself. If you think you can identify me as this famous man in dark glasses you're talking about, you're making a big mistake. I tell you, I was here in London when Vale was murdered."

"Seven people at least will join in making a composite picture of the man. They will prove together that he was you, Mr. Firmin. Let me give you one example. That ring, sir, you're wearing on your finger. You forgot to take it off when you tried to conceal your identity. One of them can describe it. Another, your walk and build. A third, he'll recognise your voice, and two other ladies will confirm it. Altogether, they'll construct your complete identity... Are you ready? Let's go."

Littlejohn and Cromwell rose, but Firmin didn't. He was weighing up the odds and now looking less sure of himself. Finally, he seemed to make up his mind.

"I guess I'd better tell you the truth. The man on the 'plane was me. But I didn't kill Vale. You can't prove that. Simply because I entered the *Carlton* by the back door doesn't mean I was out to get Vale."

"Why all the cloak-and-dagger stuff, then?"

"This is what happened. I believe you travelled on the same 'plane as Hal Vale, Superintendent, from Dublin..."

"Yes."

"Did you notice anything about him?"

"He was sulky and far from looking like a triumphant popular figure going to meet his public."

"That's the way he was when I left him in Dublin. And I'll tell you why. Before Vale and Monique Dol left London, she for the Isle of Man, he to go to Dublin to settle his affairs with Marie, Vale promised to form a film company to produce Monique's films. When he told Armstrong, who had attended to the financing of previous Monique Dol productions, there was a fearful row between him and Armstrong. Armstrong represented a syndicate, with Mauron behind it, and Armstrong said Monique was under contract to them. The truth was, however, that

Armstrong was mad about Monique, and the idea of losing her was more than he could stand."

"Was Monique, by the way, somewhat of a tartar on location?"

"She was really a little tramp, a guttersnipe. She'd always go for the highest bidder. And when she'd got all she could out of him, she'd go back to Mauron, who, in his cynical way, seemed to enjoy watching her fool one after another of them. What could you expect of her? She was the illegitimate daughter of a prompter—*un souffleur*—at the Comédie Française and *une ouvrière* a seat-attendant. Have you ever heard her say she was born to the stage? That's the way it was. She'd a lovely figure—always had—and good looks. She started as a model for photographs in the nude. Then, someone picked her up and one day, her lucky day, she came across Mauron..."

"What about Vale?"

"He was more smitten on her than on any woman I ever knew him fall for. And, believe me, I know. I've got him out of more scrapes with women than I can count. Monique must have tired of dancing to Mauron's tune, supervised by W. J. Armstrong, and decided she'd be her own boss on Vale's money. As I said, she persuaded him to start a company. That needed money. Plenty."

"Vale wasn't short of money, was he?"

Firmin sneered.

"So he thought, too. He and I had a private conference in Dublin after we'd settled Marie's affair and he told me to take all the legal steps about the company. The first thing was to get the capital. Then and there, he decided to sell stock to provide the funds. He told me to ring up W. J. Armstrong, who was the head of Mauron's banking house in London, and tell him to sell his largest holding, which was in SAHB. Société Anonyme de Huile de Bétainville. It was a speculation on which Mauron had put him. One of Mauron's own companies and it had trebled in value over four years. It made Vale rich. A cool hundred and fifty thousand pounds worth of shares. I got on the 'phone at once to W.J...."

Firmin smiled grimly.

"When I mentioned it to Armstrong there was a silence and then he laughed. 'Is Vale selling to finance his new film company?' I said that was right. 'He'd better sell something else, then. SAHB. shares aren't worth the paper they're written on. Instead of striking oil, they've found just sand, miles deep. They've stopped boring and are in liquidation...' You see, the shares were all privately subscribed and there wasn't a public quotation. Vale had depended utterly on Mauron. When I told Vale, he went like somebody mad. He rang up Cannes, Aix, Lyon—trying to get Mauron, who wasn't available. Finally, Vale went off on the next 'plane to the Isle of Man to see W. J. Armstrong."

"Leaving you behind?"

"Yes. There was only one seat to spare and Vale got it. But as soon as I'd seen him off, I realised that, if they met, there'd be murder. I followed to try to do something about it."

"Disguised?"

"If you were going with the idea of preventing violence, but were a bit behindhand, would you shout your identity from the housetops? I tried to get there incog., I can tell you. I wanted to help Vale, but I wasn't going to mix myself up in bloodshed. When I arrived and found Vale dead, I felt I'd done the wisest thing. Unfortunately, you happened to turn up on the case. Now it looks as if *I'd* done it. But I assure you, I didn't. You can put a man on my tail, even lock me up whilst you continue the investigation, but I tell you I didn't kill Vale."

Firmin paused. Then he rose and took off his dressing-gown.

"I'd better get properly dressed and come with you. On second thoughts, you'd better charge me with something and lock me up."

"Why the change of mind?"

"Because I've told you more already than is good for me. Remember what happened to W. J. Armstrong. He talked too much. And somebody silenced him for good."

11

THE WATCHER IN THE NIGHT

"Sure you won't have a drink after all this time?"

It was past one o'clock. Firmin was hoarse and sweating. Receiving no reply from the policemen, he filled-up his own glass again. In spite of the amount he had drunk, he maintained his coherence.

The flats were completely silent, except for Firmin's voice, which, under the strain, had assumed a dull monotone. Outside, a taxi passed now and then, the footsteps of a passer-by, cars hurrying home...

Littlejohn took out another pipe and slowly filled it. Cromwell had hardly spoken a word, but waited expectantly for a climax. He took his cue from Littlejohn and filled and lit his own.

"Let us get the timing quite clear, Mr. Firmin. You knocked on the staff door of the *Carlton*, someone let you in, you climbed the staff staircase, and came out on the first floor. On the corridor at the end of which was Vale's suite. Right?"

"Yes."

"Then...?"

"I waited behind the door which gave on the main corridor for a minute to make sure there was nobody about. I intended contacting Vale and trying to talk him into reason. I thought there might be some violence between him and Armstrong; violence which might end in tragedy."

"But why go to Vale's room when you knew he'd probably be down below at the cocktail party?"

"I knew nothing about any party. I expected Vale would have sent for Armstrong and that they'd be having it out. That is, if I hadn't arrived too late. When all seemed quiet, I was opening the corridor door when I heard footsteps hurrying in my direction. I slipped in the servants' room behind. W. J. Armstrong suddenly opened the door, which, fortunately, was hinged in the right direction as far as I was concerned and half-covered the doorway of the room where I was standing. He didn't see me. He disappeared down the stairs and out by the staff entrance."

"Yes... ?"

"I made sure there was nobody else about and went to Vale's suite. I'd already inspected it with McLeary to make sure it would suit Hal, so I knew where to go. When I got there, the door was ajar, the lights were on in the bedroom and the bathroom. There was complete silence. I went to the bathroom and found Vale in the bath, obviously dead. I could see how it had happened, too."

"Why didn't you raise the alarm? At first sight, didn't it appear to be suicide?"

"Do you really think that was my first impulse, Superintendent? Imagine me. I'd crept in by the back entrance, and, if you'd found the kitchen porter who'd let me in, you and the rest would have come to one conclusion, that I'd killed Vale. And, having seen Armstrong sneaking out, I was sure at the time that he'd murdered Vale, whom he hated like poison. I thought they'd had the row, and Armstrong had killed him."

"They'd had an argument whilst Vale was in his bath?"

"Why not, if Armstrong found him there? I didn't stop to think how or why W. J. had chosen such a peculiar way of murder. All I knew was I was instinctively sure he'd done it. And, if I said I'd seen him coming from the dead man's room as I arrived, nobody would have believed me. Why should they? I'd been, as you remarked, playing cloak-and-dagger. I was the one they'd suspect. I took to my heels and cautiously made off, got the next 'plane to London, as I'd planned to do if anything went wrong, and framed the best alibi I could."

"You conveniently happened to have your evening clothes with you."

"In my large case. I slipped them into a small one I had as the taxi was making its way to the airport and took it with me as hand luggage. You know all that, I gather?"

"We do. Did you see anyone on the corridor as you fled?"

"No."

"Not even Monique Dol?"

"Certainly not Monique. She was on the floor above, and I'd no time to pay her a courtesy call."

"What motive did you think people would impute to you for murdering Vale?"

"That I was in love with Marie Vale and wished to kill Vale before he could alter the will in which she inherited a fortune. You might say that perhaps nobody knew of our affair. How was I to know? You, yourself, got to know of it, didn't you? I couldn't risk it."

"I wonder why the kitchen porter didn't tell the police about the backstairs comings and goings when he heard about Vale's death."

"He's a half-witted sort of man who looks after the rubbish and swill-bins. He's not the kind who would want any contact with the police. He's scared of his own shadow. The sort of chap everybody pushes around. Had everybody been interrogated, he might have said something. I say, *might*. But he didn't."

"You still think Armstrong killed Vale?"

"No. He came by the back way because he wanted to see Vale secretly, I presume, about the phoney investment. I think he was somewhere about when the crime was committed, either hiding in Vale's room, or perhaps behind the door to the staff quarters. Like I was. I think he knew the murderer and I think he went to accuse Mauron of sending one of his strong-arm men to eliminate Vale. That wouldn't be difficult for Mauron. He has his men everywhere. Perhaps he'd someone over here watching his interests with Vale and Monique. Or, Armstrong might have 'phoned Mauron after the row with Hal Vale. I don't know. On mature consideration afterwards, I couldn't possibly imagine Armstrong killing Vale that way. He was twice as strong as Vale. All he'd need to do on finding Vale in his bath and getting insulted at what he said, was to shove him under the water and hold him there for a few minutes. Why seek out the electric razor, fit it up, and then throw it in Vale's bath?"

"To make it look like an accident."

"Why did *you* know it wasn't an accident?"

"Because Vale had just been shaved properly by the valet. Why should he do it all over again in his bath?"

"All the same, I don't see W. J. killing him like that. He had a furious temper when he was roused. He'd have pushed and held Vale under the water. I think he'd phoned Mauron and told him about Vale and his wanting to sell the shares and Mauron, as I said, arranged to have Vale bumped-off before the thing went any further. What do you think would have happened if Vale had kicked up a stink about Mauron's fraud on the Bétainville oils? It might have ruined Mauron. He's not the man to stand by and let anybody accuse him of share-pushing, especially when the shares are phoney."

"Why do you think W. J. Armstrong was shot, then?"

"Because he saw who committed the crime and went straight away to Mauron to tell him he knew all about it. Perhaps he tried a little blackmail. At any rate, we can guess who killed W. J. in Aix. It was someone in Mauron's pay, you can be sure."

"Does anyone else know about your escapade at the time of Vale's death?"

"No. Only you. If Mauron gets to know, I'd better look out. He'll want me out of the way before I can tell what I know."

"We've told nobody..."

"Are you sure?"

"Quite sure."

"Then, I've got a sporting chance. You've got a man watching the flats from the street, I see. That'll be some protection. Can you leave him there?"

"We have no man there now. I'll admit we had one on your tail earlier today, but he left when we arrived here."

For the first time Firmin looked really afraid.

"You what! I saw him posted in the doorway opposite. I looked from my bedroom window when I went in for my coat. That means someone's keeping an eye on me."

"You're mistaken, I think, Mr. Firmin. It seems somebody is watching *me*. I'm the hunted man. Someone is anxious to know just what I find out and what I do. Is the light out in your bedroom?"

"Yes."

Littlejohn crossed and entered the room. The curtains were drawn and he peeped round them cautiously. In the doorway of the block of flats opposite, he could see the glow of a cigarette and a dark shadow.

He returned to where Firmin and Cromwell were sitting in anxious silence, took up the telephone, and gave instructions for the man in the doorway opposite to be picked up for loitering.

"The man's there and he's not one of us. I think this means we'll have to arrest you, Mr. Firmin. We'll take you with us and you must make a show of reluctance as we leave the flats and bundle you in the car, just in case the man opposite gives our chaps the slip. We'll go now."

They left with Firmin between them and, as they came to the

main door to the street, Firmin acted his part very well. He argued, made as if to return, was hauled back, and bundled in the police car. As they turned the corner, Littlejohn looked back. The watcher had emerged, flung his cigarette into the darkness, and made off in the opposite direction.

"Now we shall see," said Littlejohn.

"One more thing, and we'll call it a day."

They'd tucked Firmin safely away for the night. Littlejohn picked up the 'phone.

"Ask records if they've had any case recently, or can trace one in which anybody's died in his bath by dropping in an electric razor. This method of killing seems quite a novel one for someone to think of on the spur of the moment. And, by the way, just to make sure, ask them to 'phone and see if the Paris police can do the same. The case seems to extend all over the shop. I'm damned if I don't think we ought to ask Dublin, too! Then we'll have boxed the compass. Ask Dublin, as well."

It was three o'clock when he got home to Hampstead. His wife was waiting up for him. He'd telephoned her every night since he'd left for Dublin on his wild-goose chase, but otherwise he hadn't seen her or even had time to write.

"Would you like me to cook you something, Tom?"

He realised that he hadn't had a proper meal since leaving Ireland.

The next morning at nine, Littlejohn was sitting at his desk at Scotland Yard. After his recent 'holiday' up and down the place, it was a relief to be back again. The worn, familiar furniture, the swivel chair that squeaked, the calendar sent from prison by a man called Beeton, who'd almost been tried for murder and who, after all, had proved to be a mere bigamist. The sun shone through the open window and cast a rainbow across the top of the desk as it struck the glass paperweight with an inset relief of Queen Victoria, and with which an old lady had once rendered a burglar unconscious pending the arrival of the police.

There was a card of the *Promenade des Anglais* from Nice in the morning post from the Rev. Caesar Kinrade, who was still enjoying his holiday in the flower-fields near Vence and urged Littlejohn to return quickly.

Firmin, it was reported, had spent a good night and had eaten a large breakfast. He was somewhat of an embarrassment and, for a lawyer, the police who weren't in the know about the case thought him singularly inept. He'd been charged with unlawfully entering an hotel bedroom at Douglas, Isle of Man, with intent to steal, and would have to be taken back to the Island to face the magistrates there. A bit of slow-motion about the journey and the formalities might keep him in a safe place pending confirmation, if any, of his story, or further developments in the case.

Inspector Knell, in Douglas, had already been informed of the part the half-witted kitchen porter had played in letting-in Firmin on the day of Vale's murder and they were seeking him out. Meanwhile, Firmin was happy and comfortable. He had asked for some detective stories to while away the time and then, short of someone to talk with, had asked for the loan of a tape recorder.

On the face of it, Littlejohn began to be sorry for Hal Vale. He felt sure that much of Firmin's confession was a cock-and-bull story. If Firmin hadn't actually killed Vale, he'd been on his way to do it, and found that someone else had got there first. And W. J. Armstrong... Had he been the one? Yet, Firmin had done his best to absolve Armstrong. Hardly a course of argument for a man who, with Armstrong dead, could have sheltered behind him and accused him plainly.

Telephone.

It was Records and they had heard from Paris. A message on the teleprinter about recent cases of death by electrocution in baths. There had been three reported over the past ten years. In 1953, the Comte de Porquerolles had killed himself by shaving in his bath at his home in Clichy. An obvious accident because his valet had been in the next room when it occurred and stated he had often warned the Count about the dangers of the habit. The second, in 1953, as well; an actress who'd tried to shave her armpits, with wet hands in a bath. Finally, a Monsieur Biot, who, it seemed, had plugged his shaver in a light-socket and electrocuted himself after bathing by first dropping the thing in the bath, and then trying to retrieve it by dipping his hands in the water whilst standing in a pool of his own drippings on the tiles.

The brief newspaper note of each death had been included with the teleprinter advice. The first two were banal accidents.

The third was more interesting. Littlejohn read it twice. It was dated 1957.

> Yesterday, Monsieur Alexandre Biot, a well-known theatrical agent, was electrocuted in his bath. He had been using an electric shaver, which must have slipped from his hands into the bathwater. Whilst trying to retrieve the shaver...
>
> Monsieur Biot, who occupied a flat in Rue de Clignancourt, was the friend and agent of many well-known celebrities in the theatrical and film world...

Rue de Clignancourt... Littlejohn was sure it was somewhere behind the Sacré-Coeur, Montmartre. He looked it up on the map of Paris. He was right. It was just behind the church. And across the street, the entrance to Rue du Chevalier de la Barre, where, according to the old envelope, postmarked 1957, Monique Dol had once lived.

It might have been pure coincidence. On the other hand, it might not. The departure of Monsieur Biot under tragic circumstances must have been well-known among his friends and clients in the theatre and films. The newspaper report was detailed enough and the enquiry explicit enough to reveal fully the technique of death by electric razor in a bath. Perhaps Monique Dol, a nearby neighbour of M. Biot, had remembered it.

Littlejohn was just stretching his hand to the telephone when it rang again. It was the Inspector of the Division covering Firmin's flat.

"We've got the man here we picked up in the flat doorway in accordance with your instructions last night, sir. We rang you at once, but you'd left. So we charged him and put him in the cells. He was armed, so that was easy."

"What name?"

"Smith."

"A very popular name these days."

"Yes, sir. But that's a fake. He speaks with a foreign accent. I'd guess he's French. No identity card or passport. Nothing on him except his cigarettes, a lighter, some keys, a gun, a pencil, and three bottles of pills; pep-pills, dyspepsia tablets and multi-vitamin capsules. He says he was waiting there for a friend. That's all we can get out of him. He gave our men a run for their money. Broke away and beat it, and when they caught up with him— luckily one of the detective constables was a half-miler—he put up a fight. They had to handcuff him."

"You'd better bring him over, then. I think I've met him before. All those pills seem to ring a bell!"

"What's it all about, sir?"

"The murder of Hal Vale. It's becoming an international *cause célèbre*..."

"Beg pardon, sir."

"Just my joke. Bring him along, please."

Then Littlejohn asked for Douglas police, Inspector Knell.

"Hullo, Knell..."

"Hullo, sir. Are you ringing me, or am I ringing you? I'd just put in a call..."

He'd no time to ask about Monique Dol. Knell was full of it.

"Monica Dol's left by the first 'plane for London, sir. It seems there was a 'phone call from France for her at seven this morning. As soon as she'd spoken, she packed a bag, ordered a taxi, and went off to the airport. She booked to London, but as there isn't a 'plane to London till afternoon, she's routed via Manchester to arrive in London at 11.30."

"What was the message, Knell? Did you ask the operator at the hotel?"

"It was the night-porter. Trust him to listen-in. He said all the man at the other end said was, ' Come to me right away. I'll explain when I see you. I'll meet you at the 'plane.' That was all. It was in French, but the hall-porter knew a bit of French and could make it out. What shall I do?"

"I'll look after it, old man. Thanks for dealing with it. I'll keep you advised."

Littlejohn telephoned to the airport police.

"Do you wish us to detain her, sir?"

"No. She'll presumably be getting the next 'plane to Nice. When is that?"

"Noon. Viscount. That is, if the Manchester 'plane gets in on schedule."

"Right. Please let me know... Wait... You'd better reserve a seat for me, too. Same 'plane. But I must be aboard before she arrives. She'll presumably travel First. Save me a seat in a quiet spot in the Tourist section, then. I don't want her to see me."

"You can depend on us, sir..."

Then, Nice.

Dorange was luckily in his office.

"*Comment-ça-va...?*"

A wave of nostalgia. Littlejohn could see his old friend in his little office in the Sûreté at Nice, his jacket draped over the back of his chair, a *Gitanes* cigarette in his mouth. And outside, the hot sunshine, the flower market, the fabulous blue Mediterranean...

"Monique is on her way to see her *oncle* again. She'll leave by the noon Viscount for Nice."

"We'll be there."

"So will I."

"You, too. Good; we'll meet you both."

"I'll be last off the 'plane and not until Monique and Mauron have gone. He's meeting her."

"I have some news for you, too. Mauron was not speaking from Messina when I rang him after Armstrong's murder. He was on his motor-boat in Cannes Bay."

"How come?"

"We called on the radio-telephone station at Grasse. The operator in charge at the time Mauron was supposed to be in Messina was rather reluctant to talk. Apparently the matter had been satisfactorily arranged between him and Mauron. However, it was also satisfactorily settled between the operator and me, as well. He told the truth. That Mauron had spoken to me from his small boat in Cannes Bay."

"So that demolishes his alibi for the time of Armstrong's death."

"The next thing is what to do for the best. Arrest Mauron? I'm afraid not. We must first dovetail the Isle of Man murder with that in Aix. You are coming over here again on the trail of Monique?"

"I've booked a seat on the next 'plane, as I said. She'll also be travelling by it if what I hear is correct."

"*A tout à l'heure*, then?"

"*A tout à l'heure.*"

A knock on the door and an attendant entered.

"They've brought over the man Smith who was arrested for loitering and carrying firearms last night, sir."

"Send them in, please."

Two plain-clothes men arrived with Smith between them.

"Well, well. Good morning, Mr. Smith. Haven't we met before?"

It was Augustin Meunier, Monique Dol's advertising agent! Meunier looked shocking. He wasn't much at the best of times and now was more hatchet-faced than ever. His dark, heavy beard had grown overnight and he hadn't had a shave. He looked as if they'd picked him up sleeping on the Embankment.

Meunier was furious.

"This is no joke. You'll be laughing at the other side of your face by the time I've finished with this business..."

His Franco-American accent was more pronounced than ever.

"We won't waste any of your time, then, Mr. Smith. By the way, what *is* your name? Smith or Meunier?"

"Never mind that. What's the meaning of my being picked up and held in gaol all night. I was simply in a doorway lighting a cigarette. When I emerged, I was seized and rough-housed by the police."

"Why were you carrying a revolver?"

"I always do. I travel in some queer places."

"I'm sure you do. Do you hold a permit for it?"

"No. I forgot to get one when I came here from France."

"You were keeping an eye on Mr. Firmin, I believe. You'd been in the doorway opposite his flat for more than an hour. It takes you a long time to light a cigarette."

"I tell you I'd just stepped in the doorway to light a cigarette. Why should I be tailing Firmin?"

"Doubtless under instructions from Paul Mauron."

"Who's he?"

"Come, come, Mr. Smith. As an advertising man, aren't you forgetting one or two details about your employer. Paul Mauron is the divorced husband of Monique Dol, isn't he? Remember?"

"What has he to do with me being in a doorway lighting a cigarette last night?"

"That's for you to tell me. Meanwhile, until you make up your mind, you'll be held in gaol. You'll go from here to a magistrate, who will remand you on a charge of loitering with intent, and of being illegally in possession of firearms. There will be no bail."

"Here, you can't do that to me! It'll kill me. I've stomach ulcers and only one lung. They took away my medicines last night and

I'm a lot worse this morning. If I die on your hands, there'll be a hell of a stink, I can tell you."

"We'll risk it, Mr. Smith. You can see the police doctor, if you wish. He'll fix you up and make you comfortable."

"I don't want your blasted police doctor. I'm in the hands of specialists."

"The best way of keeping alive, then, Mr. Smith, seems to be for you to tell me exactly what you were doing skulking in a doorway keeping an eye on Firmin's flat, armed, and apparently ready to do him harm when you could get at him."

Meunier plunged into a nervous crisis. His hair was too short-clipped for him to tear, but he did his best. Finally, one of his attendants thrust him into a chair and gave him a glass of water.

"Behave yourself, Smith."

"I wasn't skulking in doorways and..."

"Did you attend Hal Vale's funeral yesterday, by the way?"

"Yes. And at this rate, it will be mine next."

"Why didn't Miss Dol go, too? I hear she wasn't there. I'd say she missed a fine chance of some good publicity."

"She wouldn't go. It seems they weren't so friendly at the time he died."

"That's a strange tale. They were together at the cocktail-party just before."

"They got out of each other's company as soon as they could. Agostini, the director of the film, said they never spoke to each other all the way from the airport. He was the only one who was pleased when Hal died. He said the way the two of them were carrying-on, the film would be a washout."

"So you represented Miss Dol at Hal's funeral?"

"Yes."

"Not Firmin?"

"Firmin was Hal Vale's man."

"Did Monique tell you to keep an eye on him whilst he was in London?"

"Sorta."

"She told you to let her know if I, or any of the police contacted him and to find out what it was all about."

"She's told you?"

"No. But I guessed. You were so anxious to do as she ordered, that you'd have used a gun on Firmin to get out of him what he'd told us. Well, you'll not be able to report to her what went on. She's disappeared again."

Meunier put his head in his hands and slumped over the desk.

"Not again! Not again! Has she bolted off to Mauron again? Well, that's torn it. The film's off."

"It's off in any case. Who's to finance it? Vale's dead and so is W. J. Armstrong. Mauron's not likely to find the money now."

"Why?"

"Mauron isn't interested in films or anything else here just now. He has bigger things to think of."

"Such as…?"

"You'll learn soon enough. Meanwhile, have you anything to tell me about the death of Hal Vale, Mr. Smith?"

"For God's sake don't call me Mr. Smith any more! It's driving me nuts your being sarcastic with me. It upsets my ulcers. You know my name. I guess I said it was Smith sort of instinctive…"

"Where were you when Vale died?"

"What again? The Isle of Man police asked me at least a dozen times. I was in the bar, at the cocktail party, with dozens of people who knew me and will give me alibis."

"Do you often carry a gun?"

"As I said, I get in some queer places."

"You were Miss Dol's bodyguard?"

"Yes. It was in my interests to keep her alive. She paid me well."

"*She* paid you? Wasn't it Mauron?"

"If he did pay me, it was through Monique."

"Nothing more to tell us?"

"No. Want me to make something up? By the way, can I have my pills? I'm on a strict schedule with pills and if I miss I feel bad."

"Give him his pills, constable, as soon as you get back."

"And do I go free now? I've nothing else to tell you."

"No. You'll be brought before the bench in the morning. Meanwhile, you'll be our guest. You can have your pills or see the police doctor, and I don't want to hear any more about your ulcers or your one lung, Mr. Meunier. Good morning."

And with that, Littlejohn went off to the airport.

12

THE WOMAN'S WAY

There seemed to be more traffic at London airport than ever. It was the high season of the holidays and the place was like bedlam. Loud-speakers bawling, people rushing here and there trying to sort themselves out after late connections, large parties of trippers wringing their hands and almost rioting because their 'planes hadn't arrived or had been cancelled. Littlejohn's Viscount was half-an-hour late in starting because there was so much traffic in the air that they had to wait their turn.

It had been a roasting day in London. Over Lyon the weather changed, they ran into thunderstorms, two women had hysterics, and two Italians exchanged fisticuffs. They touched-down at Nice an hour and a half behind schedule. The sun was shining and you'd have thought it had been doing so for weeks. Littlejohn got out in a blaze of sunlight and the air was vibrating with the heat. He watched Monique Dol leave the 'plane and meet Mauron's chauffeur on the parterre of the arrival side. Then he left the 'plane himself.

There was no reception-party this time. Littlejohn felt thankful for that. It was always a bit embarrassing. Instead, a small, slim swarthy figure in a pearl-grey alpaca suit dashed up to him.

"Superintendent Littlejohn? My name's Pellepuits. I'm helping Inspector Dorange. He's been detained..."

Pellepuits! What a name! And what a man! He was like a jumping-Jack. He seized Littlejohn's bag and made off for the exit as though the devil were after him. Following him was like ploughing your way through hot wool. The air was thick with the heat.

"No need to bother about customs or passports. I've fixed it. Is this your first trip to Nice?"

So much for that! Littlejohn swabbed his forehead and tried to keep up with his guide, who, by now, was already sitting in a little car with the engine humming in the rear, waiting for him.

"Have you had lunch on the 'plane?"

"Yes, thanks. We struck a thunderstorm and most of it ended on the floor. All the same, I'd like to get on."

Pellepuits looked amused.

"You can't work without food. No, no. After a long journey... What do you fancy?"

Littlejohn wondered whether or not Pellepuits was Dorange's senior officer or an underling. He was so aggressive and full of beans that he seemed to be running the show.

"A sandwich will do."

"We'll go back to the airport bar, then. Do you want ham or roast beef?"

"Get a couple of roast beef and I'll eat them on the way. Are we going to Cannes to join the Inspector?"

"No. He left the commissariat at ten o'clock and said he'd be back in time to meet your 'plane. When he didn't turn up, I thought I'd better come myself. He must have been delayed."

Delayed! Two hours behind time! Most unlike Dorange.

Pellepuits leapt from the car and vanished inside the airport. He was soon back with a couple of long crisp rolls full of beef.

"I told them to put butter on them. Most Englishmen like butter, don't they?"

It was ridiculous! Littlejohn had had enough.

"Whereabouts in Cannes do you think Inspector Dorange will be?"

"I've no idea. I rang up the police there when he didn't turn up, but they said he'd not called on them. He'll be all right. He always is."

"You're *au fait* with the case, I presume?"

"Yes. The death of an Englishman called Armstrong at Aix, you mean? Yes. It seems to have been a *crime passionnel*. The film star, Monique Dol, was involved. I think Inspector Dorange must have come upon some new features in the case. He..."

"What features?"

"I can't say. He's not reported yet. He was waiting for you to arrive and compare notes."

"We'd better make for Cannes, then. I think I know where he might be."

"But..."

"Turn and let's make for Cannes."

Poor Pellepuits! He seemed bewildered but he did as he was told and recovered his spirits at once.

"We'll take the coast road through Cannes. You'll be able to enjoy the sea view, then, and I can point out some places of interest on the way."

Littlejohn let him talk away. He couldn't take it seriously. He was on a job and Dorange was missing, and yet in the heat and with everyone dressed in holiday clothes or nothing at all, he became infected with the holiday feeling and sat torpidly in his seat watching the world go by, and now and then almost falling asleep.

"We're just entering Antibes. I shan't go through the town. You can see that later. There's a side-road here. It won't be so busy and I can crack on a bit of speed."

"What for?"

Littlejohn wasn't being funny. It was just that Pellepuits didn't seem in the least anxious about Dorange. They might have been going to join him on a picnic. His confidence infected Littlejohn. Nothing ever happened to Dorange, he'd said.

They tore along a little narrow lane with villas on either side. Now and then, they came across a car travelling in the opposite direction and Pellepuits hooted it out of the way. The place was ablaze with geraniums, bougainvillaea, and other flowers Littlejohn had never come across before. Orange trees, too, with little oranges hanging on them.

"That's Juan... Nice, isn't it?"

The picnic continued.

"That's the Ali Khan's house and the one you can see up above us on the right belongs to the murdered man."

"Armstrong, you mean?"

"Yes."

"Pull up. I'd like to see it. Do you think Inspector Dorange might have called there?"

"I'm sure I don't know. That's the way up, just past the hole they're digging in the road. Shall we take it?"

"Yes."

Pellepuits turned right and snaked furiously uphill. There was a deep ditch running with water on the right and, now and then, Littlejohn closed his eyes, sure that Pellepuits was going to land them in it. Eventually, they pulled up at some expensive wrought-iron gates, followed a gravel path, and drew up in front of a villa which looked like a small country club. A wide terrace sloping away to lawns with flower-beds. All neat and well-kept. Deep vegetation fringing the terrace. Mimosas, cacti, orange and lemon trees, a tennis-court...

Pellepuits bounced out of the car.

"Shall I ring the bell?"

The front door was like that of a convent. Thick oak, covered with iron studs and a Judas-window in the middle.

A man in a striped waistcoat answered, after eyeing them through the Judas. He might have been expecting them. A heavy, shambling, middle-aged fellow, like a peasant who had been promoted to *maître d'hotel* because there wasn't anyone else available.

Littlejohn took charge.

"Is this the late Mr. Armstrong's villa?"

"Yes. He was buried yesterday at Antibes."

"Are you the only one in the place?"

"Me and my wife. We're packing our things and going to a new job."

He was a shifty chap, with dark, sneaky eyes and a bald head. There was two days' growth of black beard on his cheeks.

"Had any callers today?"

"Yes. An Inspector of police called about eleven."

"We're from the police, too."

Pellepuits piped up to impress the man with his duty towards them.

"Well, I've nothing to tell. I said that to the Inspector."

"What did he want?"

"He had Mr. Armstrong's keys. Said they'd found them on the body. He asked where the safe was kept. I told him behind a picture in the study. Then he said I'd to show him where it was. He opened it with the key and some numbers he'd got in Mr. Armstrong's diary, which he also had with him."

"Did you stay with him whilst he opened it?"

"Yes."

"Well?"

"All the papers had vanished, but the money wasn't touched."

"How did you know about the papers?"

"I used to go in with Mr. Armstrong when he got the money for the wages and upkeep of the villa. I often saw inside the safe.

The top shelf was full of papers. They'd gone when the Inspector opened it."

"Perhaps Mr. Armstrong took them with him."

"No, he didn't. He called here and slept the night the evening before he was killed. Before he left in the morning, he opened the safe to give me the usual money. He took and handed me the cash and put some more papers in. Then he locked it and, soon after, he left. He was a decent boss. I'm sorry it's come to this."

"Did Inspector Dorange ask you about the papers?"

"I told him what I told you."

"Anything else?"

"He asked if there was anybody else with him when he came here for the last time. There wasn't, I said. So he wanted to know how Mr. Armstrong seemed. I said very cheerful."

"And then...?"

"I told him, like I told you, that he stayed here the night before he died, and that before he left in the morning he rang up Mauron's flat at Aix-en-Provence. I got the call for him. It was a woman answered. I don't know what they said. I'd my duties to attend to."

"Were there any other calls in or out before Mr. Armstrong left for Aix?"

"The Inspector asked that, as well. Mr. Armstrong tried to get a call to a villa at Super-Cannes... *Montjouvain*, I think it was. But there was no reply."

"Is that all?"

"Should there be more?"

"You think the place was burgled and the safe robbed?"

"It must have been. I don't know when, but I'm sure somebody must have had the keys of the front door and the safe and known the numbers to open the lock of the safe. There wasn't a sign of forcing the door, and nobody could open the safe without a key and leave it looking as if it hadn't been touched."

"What kind of papers were they? Documents?"

"They looked like bonds, if you ask me."

"How do you know what bonds are like?"

"You might not think it, but my own father, who was a wealthy farmer in the Basses-Alpes, put a lot of his money in French Rentes and used to keep them in a box under the floor. He used to take them out now and then just to look them over. When the franc was devalued, years ago that was, the Rentes went down in value, too, and it drove the old man off his head. He ended up in an asylum. That's why I've had to come out to work as a servant. So I know a bit about bonds."

"Were there many of them?"

"A whole wad, tied-up with pink tape."

"You told the Inspector that, too?"

"Yes."

"Anything more?"

"Yes. He asked if there was a way from here to La Californie, in Cannes, without going back on the main road. I told him there was, and showed him. It's up the hill, then you turn left, keep along the road, which is a bit narrow, but quite passable. Carry on till you come to a main crossing. Take that road and it winds up straight to the Observatory at Super-Cannes."

"Thanks."

"'*Service!*'"

They carried on as directed.

"Where are we going, sir?"

"*Montjouvain*. I'll show you the way once we get to the main road..."

In the heat of the afternoon everybody seemed to be enjoying a siesta. Workmen mending the road were stretched out on the grass verge, some asleep, others smoking or drinking wine from bottles.

Montjouvain looked deserted, but when they reached the gravelled terrace at the front door, a chauffeur emerged from a small red sports car. He was in uniform and an unpleasant-looking customer into the bargain. His nose had been broken and badly set and, judging from his powerful physique, perhaps he was one of Mauron's bodyguards as well as his driver.

"What do you want?"

"Is Monsieur Mauron at home?"

"Why?"

"No reason to tell you. Is he in?"

"I'll have to see. Wait here."

He hurried indoors and was soon back.

"What name?"

"Superintendent Littlejohn and Brigadier Pellepuits..."

"He said if it was Superintendent Littlejohn, you were to be shown in. Anybody else was to wait here."

"We'll both go in..."

"No, you won't..."

They found themselves looking down the barrel of a rifle which the man had taken from the car.

"You stay here, as I said."

He waved Pellepuits aside with the gun.

"The Superintendent will go right inside. Knock on the door in the corner there, and enter."

No use arguing. Littlejohn crossed to the study he knew well from his last visit, and knocked and entered. All the time the chauffeur covered the two of them from the doorway with the rifle.

Inside, Mauron was sitting at the table and Dorange was opposite in a chair, smoking a cigarette. In Mauron's hand was a tommy-gun.

"Good afternoon, Superintendent. I was surprised when Valentin, the chauffeur, described you. I thought you were in the Isle of Man. But, somehow, I'd a premonition we'd soon be seeing you."

Littlejohn ignored him. Mauron seemed so pleased with some triumph or other he was enjoying that he was purring like a cat.

"Hullo, old man. What brings you here?"

Dorange gave him a wry smile.

"You see, I'm somewhat under restraint..."

Mauron smiled grimly.

"Don't mind me. Talk together just as if I were not here. It's nice to see old friends meet. Especially when it's for the last time."

The voice was icy. Mauron was still smiling, however. He rang the bell and the servant in the striped waistcoat appeared. He was trundling his cocktail vehicle with him and might have been dumb, for he never spoke a word.

"Give them a drink, Adolphe. What will it be, gentlemen?"

Dorange didn't seem to be bothering about what was a dangerous situation.

"*Deux Pernods.*"

The man handed them the drinks.

"It doesn't seem much use drinking each other's health, gentlemen, in the circumstances. Still, please yourselves."

Dorange took a sip of his drink and sighed.

"M. Mauron is playing at heroics, Littlejohn. He tells me that Monique Dol is in her room upstairs, and when I ask him to hand her over to us, he answers by saying he's going to kill me."

"Both of you, now. I want you out of the way. You've disturbed me quite enough."

"We called at W. J. Armstrong's villa, Dorange. The caretaker said you'd been there and from what he told me, too, I gathered you were here."

"Sorry, I didn't meet your 'plane, but M. Mauron and I have had a long talk and, after it, he couldn't bear me to leave him."

Mauron listened, smiling still, without a word.

"I accused Mauron of burgling Armstrong's safe to recover the bonds. It seems W. J. had somehow learned that Mauron's Bank was on the verge of going bust, and had helped himself to negotiable securities in London office to be sure he wasn't left in the lurch. For that, M. Mauron says he shot him. So, I am shortly going to leave here and M. Mauron is going to accompany me. He seems to think differently. But we shall see."

"We shall see, my friend."

Mauron wagged the gun.

"I came here this morning to discuss matters with M. Mauron, after I got your message. I'm sorry I couldn't get away to meet you at the airport. M. Mauron seems in a melodramatic mood. Miss Dol has arrived, looking somewhat the worse for wear after a rough air trip, M. Mauron tells me."

"Have you seen her?"

"No. She is in her room, I gather from M. Mauron, and he won't have her disturbed."

Mauron lit a cigarette with one hand. His coolness had not deserted him in the situation. He wore a light suit and a blue tie. Every hair was in place, every gesture calm and studied.

"And now, gentlemen, suppose we get to business. I've allowed you to greet each other and exchange courtesies. I want to know why you wish to see Miss Dol."

Littlejohn took another sip of his drink.

"Because she murdered Hal Vale, M. Mauron. I want to ask her some questions."

"If you can convince me that she's the guilty party, maybe I will arrange for you to meet her and hear what she has to say about it. Meanwhile, you can tell me why you suspect her."

"First, by process of elimination. Alibis, explanations, studying the characters of various suspects, questioning them, finding out their movements of late, have lead us to Miss Dol. One suspect has already been murdered. You yourself seem to have accounted for W. J. Armstrong…"

"But who is to say that *he* didn't murder Vale? Getting himself killed afterwards is no proof."

"The method of killing intrigued me most. It is a woman's way. The way of a woman who didn't carry a gun, who felt herself too weak or fastidious to use a knife, who wasn't strong enough to hold Vale under the water long enough to drown him, or to strangle him. A woman scorned, who wanted him dead, but who could find no way of killing him. Then, she suddenly remembered something. A way a neighbour had once met his death..."

"Others could equally have done it that way. Armstrong, for instance."

"Armstrong wasn't the type to try electrocution. He'd have used a gun. Or else, being a powerful man, would have held Vale down in the bath till he drowned. Besides, who better than a woman, used to Vale's bedroom, his mistress, in fact, would have known about the electric shaver he always had about the place?"

"I'm afraid you'll have to be more convincing than that, Littlejohn, before I let you see Monique. You've no proof at all."

"I sense from the atmosphere, monsieur, that you are finding my colleague and me an embarrassment. And I see from your present spectacular behaviour that you are even contemplating killing us..."

"A correction, Littlejohn. Not contemplating... *about* to kill you. That is finally settled. I expected you to call here and you haven't let me down. Otherwise, I would have killed Dorange long ago."

"In that case, the matter seems plain. What more proof could we need? You've guilt written all over you."

"Perhaps I have. But Monique hasn't. She's sleeping peacefully upstairs, I hope. She's not like a guilty person."

"I think it needs a conscience, M. Mauron, or else a great fear, to make one feel guilty. Miss Dol has no conscience whatever. I have never come across a more ruthless and calculating woman. As for fear. As long as you are alive and she can run to you when she's in trouble, she'll have none of that either. One of the reasons you killed Armstrong was that he was a menace to her. The other, of course, was that it was reported to you that he'd taken your bearer bonds to recompense him for loss of office when your bank goes broke, which, I believe may occur at any time."

"I've recovered the bonds, as you doubtless know."

"Yes. A burglar, as well as a banker."

Mauron shrugged.

"I already had a key to Armstrong's safe and found the combination in his diary when I last saw him in Aix."

"Dead."

"As you say, dead."

"As you're going to kill us, you may as well tell us about the bank. I do believe you've been living on your depositors' money—running yachts, villas, women, dabbling in high finance, putting on a show, for years..."

"If you adopt such a tone of contempt with me, Littlejohn, I shall kill you at once. One thing I can do to punish you, if I wish, is curtail your already short spell of life. Of course, I live on my depositors' money. It is my due for accepting it. I pay them interest and, if my speculations are successful—and they soon will be—they'll get their capital back when they ask for it. If not, I shall confiscate what is left and take my leave."

"With Miss Dol..."

"With or without her doesn't concern you. I will tell you, however, in the circumstances. It will probably be without. She is very sweet and we have similar tastes, but, of late, she has been a nuisance to me. I owe it to her that the pair of you are here now, trying to hound me into gaol. I cannot afford to repeat this performance. I'm getting too old and want a quiet life. I think Monique will have to go, much as it grieves me. And, most trying of all, she has become too promiscuous and seems to have tired of me a little. Every man she meets seems to become her lover, and then when she gets in trouble, she runs to me. As I said, I want peace at my time of life."

"And Hal Vale. Was *he* a nuisance to you?"

"Undoubtedly. You see, Monique seems to have found me too old to do anything but find her money and get her out of scrapes. She calls me *mon oncle*. Which is a ridiculous and undignified name... almost as bad as the term cuckold. She had persuaded Vale to finance her films instead of me. She was to marry him and, to put it vulgarly, leave me in the lurch. Vale had heavy investments with me and considerable deposits in my firm. He was a greedy man and I offered him the bait of high interest and capital improvement. Armstrong, who was insanely in love with Monique, had no more sense than to play a trump-card—or he thought it was one—by telling Vale he would never get his capital back from me for the film finance. That made Vale annoyed. He looked like causing a public scandal. So, both he and Armstrong were dangerous to me. I couldn't trust them. However, I only needed to deal with Armstrong. Vale must have had other enemies. One of them did the job for me."

"As a matter of fact, quite a swarm descended on him on the day he died. Two men and Monique Dol, in fact. The two men found the crime committed for them when they arrived. Monique had got there first."

"You are in the privileged position of men about to die and using that, you asked me, Littlejohn, to tell you about my Armstrong affair. I've told you. It's now your turn to tell me how you came upon the idea that Monique killed Vale. I give you just as long as it takes you to explain it all. And then I shall shoot you both. Please don't think something will occur to prevent me. My servants have instructions to keep all intruders away, even if they've to use violence. As you see, by pressing this trigger, I can eliminate the pair of you if either of you so much as moves a finger to save yourselves."

Mauron lit another cigarette with one hand, crossed his legs, inserted his monocle, and smiled blandly.

"Please begin, Littlejohn. You've exactly ten minutes."

13

THE FIRING SQUAD

The silence seemed to last an age. Dorange didn't appear at all upset. He was looking out of the open window placidly, almost wistfully, as though bidding farewell to the lovely Mediterranean, which was a part of him and which he had served so well. The sun was shining and all the noises of the town below seemed to blend into one hum. Cars passing nearby hooted as they turned the corner of the road which wound up to the Observatory.

Littlejohn was unperturbed, too. The initial shock had gone, leaving him quite calm. He wondered what his wife would do when she heard. That was the worst part of it...

On the bank above the great wrought-iron gates, the chauffeur was standing with his rifle, pretending to hunt for birds. Actually, his attention wasn't on the tree tops, but on the villa and the road below. Also, he didn't look the type who might be interested in shooting thrushes.

You had to hand it to Mauron. He never missed a trick. He'd actually posted a sentry on the house, like some tinpot South American dictator, to see that nobody disturbed him and his plans.

From the courtyard of the villa, a gravel path wound upward

through the trees to a leafy grotto, almost like the votive spot of some ancient sylvan god. There was a statue there of a satyr and in the middle of a rough-cast wall, like a rustic altar, was a lion's head spouting water.

"I suppose you both think you ought not to be executed without a trial. Let me say that you have both been on trial for some time. Very little that you have done has gone unnoticed by me or my associates. You have tried to ruin and kill me. I am now in the position of judge, I find you guilty, and you are both sentenced to death."

Dorange shrugged his shoulders in a pitying gesture.

"You silly little monomaniac! Do you think you'll get away with this? My men know where we are. They'll be here in an hour."

"They won't find you. The furniture has been sheeted, the place will be empty, even dusty, my friend. There will be no trace of recent occupancy. My private 'plane is at Mandelieu airport. We will leave quietly. I don't propose to hide your bodies, even. You have plenty of enemies, the pair of you. Your body, Littlejohn, will be found in the Thames. You'll like that, I know. And yours, my dear Dorange, in the river at St. Martin-du-Var. There was a matter of some dope smuggling there last month, and when you arrested the culprits, they swore to kill you when they got out. One of them was found not guilty and released from Marseille last week..."

"You've thought it all out, Mauron."

"I always do."

"Even Hal Vale's death."

"I had nothing to do with that."

"He was going to marry your mistress."

Mauron shrugged.

"It has happened before. Mere marriages of convenience."

"You always regarded her as your wife. Even though she divorced you and married again."

"I told you. Mere matters of convenience. She and I could not do without each other. And that will be all about Miss Dol, if you please. I don't care to discuss her with you."

Littlejohn took a cigarette from his case and lit it.

"Don't try any tricks, Littlejohn. I'm glad you didn't. I'm too old a hand at the game to fall for that."

"Did Armstrong try it at Aix?"

"Are you still harping on why and how I dealt with Armstrong?"

"Yes. You weren't in Messina when Inspector Dorange telephoned you. You were on your speed-boat in Cannes. You expected a message informing you that W. J. Armstrong had been found dead in your flat. You made arrangements to receive it. I have no doubt that if your yacht *was* in Messina at the time, you had all that arranged, too. Plenty of people would have sworn you were aboard."

"You are right. They would, if I'd wished it."

"Armstrong made a mistake in telling Vale, in an outburst of malicious rage, that his holdings in SAHB, your African oil undertaking, were worthless. He could have done you no greater wrong. One breath of doubt about your integrity, M. Mauron, would bring ruin on you. Your financial pack of cards would collapse."

"That isn't correct. SAHB are not worthless. The oil drillings were a failure, but we found much richer mineral deposits on the land. So, you see..."

"Vale didn't think that. He believed Armstrong. I'd say Armstrong was near the mark. You'll never admit ruin. You think yourself too clever for that. Vale thought he was almost ruined and he hurried to the Isle of Man from Dublin to ask Monique Dol about it. She always seemed to be in your confidence. After all, he knew *you* were *mon oncle* to her..."

For the first time the fixed smile left Mauron's face.

"Don't be impertinent, Littlejohn. As I said before, I ought to kill you for that without more ado."

"Do so, then. You will never know then all we've discovered and all I've placed on record at Scotland Yard. Or perhaps you will now arrange to blow the Yard sky-high and destroy my notes. A man as thorough as you, M. Mauron."

Paul Mauron was smiling again, teeth bared like an animal.

"Continue, Littlejohn. The more you tell me, the more I shall be forearmed."

"Vale rushed over to the Isle of Man to see Monique Dol. On the way from the reception at the airport, he didn't speak to her and at the cocktail party at the *Carlton*, in Douglas, he hurried her away for a private talk. We'll never know what was said. At least, he must have told Miss Dol that the idea of his marrying her and financing her future films was off. Perhaps her association with you had finally filled him with distaste. I think he must have threatened her and handled her violently, too. He was drunk by then and in the mood for creating a scandal which might have ruined Miss Dol's career for good."

"He quarrelled with her, struck her, told her he would tell the press as soon as he could about her and me, and what he called my frauds, which was entirely fictitious. She fled to me for help. That is all. I sent her back to answer any questions you might think would help you in the murder case. It seems you weren't satisfied."

"No. She told us nothing of any use. But a most complicated pattern of comings and goings was established around the time of Vale's death. I can only assume he quarrelled with her and struck her as they went up to their rooms and that she ran from him and locked herself in her suite. Vale, by now drunk, telephoned to her and asked to see her again. I don't know why. Perhaps the whisky he'd taken had made him more violent, or maybe amorous. At any rate, she promised to go to him. But not for a reconciliation. She is a passionate woman, who does not forgive insults..."

"Yes?"

"She looked around for some weapon with which to kill him. She found nothing. Then, an idea struck her. A friend and neighbour of hers, a Monsieur Biot, had died in his bath from electrocution. Vale had just told her he was in his bath. She was not strong enough to drown him in it, but she remembered a better way. She knew Vale used an electric razor. After all, she was already his mistress and knew all about his bedroom and his toilet equipment..."

Mauron frowned, his monocle dropped and dangled on its cord, but he made no comment.

"Vale had told her he would leave the door ajar for her. She hurried to his room, picked up his razor, went in the bathroom and, before Vale realised what was happening, she'd plugged it in, and flung it in the bath. The job was done, just as it was in the unfortunate case of M. Biot. Then she fled to you."

"I ought in justification of Monique to say, however, Littlejohn, that she told me when she entered Vale's suite, she had no thoughts of killing him. He stung her to insane fury by the abuse he heaped upon her for her association with me, for making a fool of him, and for being what he called 'a tramp—anybody's woman'. I admit, you see, that she killed him, as you will not survive to tell the tale. I congratulate you. Is that all? Time is passing."

"Not quite all. W. J. Armstrong, after telling Vale in hot blood about the worthless shares, got cold feet. He was in love with Monique Dol, too, and was perhaps afraid Vale might do her some harm. Or else, he was curious to know Vale's reaction to the tale he'd told to Firmin. Perhaps Vale would break with Monique and she might turn to W. J. on the rebound. She seems to have been a great one for the rebound! W. J. entered by the back door of the *Carlton* to avoid publicity, which he abhorred. A shy man, would you say, Mauron?"

"He kept out of the way of the press. There was too much buried in his past for him to fancy the limelight. Go on..."

"W. J. had some idea of going to Vale's room and waiting there for him. Instead, he found the door open and Vale dead. But on his way there, he saw Monique Dol in the corridor. W. J. knew then who'd killed Vale. Armstrong fled the way he'd come, but when his panic subsided, he decided that he'd found a way of keeping Monique from telling you why Vale had behaved so violently. He rang her up, but found that she had fled, too. He knew where. He followed her. He was too late. She'd already told you, but he didn't know that. By the time he reached Cannes, you had gone. So, he went to Aix. There he found the police with Miss Dol and before he could get her to himself, she had returned to the Isle of Man on your advice. He found you in her flat. You'd received a message before your yacht sailed and were waiting for him. He'd not only betrayed you to Vale, and helped himself to your bonds in case he needed to bolt or the bank crashed, but he knew who killed Hal Vale, too. So you shot him."

"True. You were both here when the telephone message arrived; remember? There's one question I wish to ask before I dispose of you. When and why did you begin to suspect Monique?"

"When it suddenly dawned on me that she never spoke of Vale's having committed suicide. When she saw her hideous method of killing him at work and Vale dead in his bath, she was too panic-stricken to give the alarm and pretend she'd found him dead from accident or suicide. She fled. She never mentioned accident or suicide when we interviewed her. She knew he'd been murdered, had it fixed on her mind by the horror of the scene, and seemed to assume that everybody else thought it was murder, too."

Dorange was silent. He was watching the gate and the man on duty there with his rifle leaning against a tree as he lit a cigarette.

"Take one from the box on the table, Dorange," said Mauron as the little Frenchman thrust his hand in his coat pocket.

Dorange smiled and shrugged, lit his cigarette from a lighter near the cigarette-box, and puffed out a languid cloud of blue smoke which slowly spread and then vanished through the open window. Outside, they could hear the birds crooning in the dovecote and, in the stillness, the splash of the water from the lion's mouth in the pool below.

Littlejohn glanced across the garden. It was with difficulty that he controlled himself. It was like a mirage! The Rev. Caesar Kinrade appeared at the gate of the villa, slowly looked around him, climbed the upward winding little side-path to the rustic altar, and disappeared among the shrubs. The man on guard looked flabbergasted at the sight of the old white-bearded parson in gaiters and shovel hat. He'd never seen his like before. He gathered up his rifle and hastily followed him. It was all done so quickly that Mauron hadn't observed it. He was busy talking.

"Surely there's no more of this. Anything else would merely be playing for time."

"Just one more matter. There was another would-be murderer on the spot. Firmin, Vale's lawyer, who was in love with Marie Vale, shortly to be free from Hal by their divorce becoming absolute. He wished to kill Vale before he could alter his will and leave all he had to Monique in place of Marie. Firmin, in turn, saw W. J. Armstrong in flight from the scene. Firmin, under pressure, told us. For that, he almost lost his life at the hands of another of your thugs, Meunier, Miss Dol's bodyguard, whom we happened to pick up, however, before he could do any harm. He'd had instructions to keep an eye on Firmin, who, for some reason, you or Miss Dol suspected knew more than was good for you."

"Meunier wouldn't have killed Firmin unless Firmin had been foolish. He had instructions to keep watch on Firmin, who was somewhat of a snake, and report to Monique. If Firmin contacted the police, Meunier was to get to know why and if necessary give Firmin a work-over. Meunier is somewhat of an expert..."

Mauron rose slowly and took up the gun from the table.

"Both of you go and stand with your faces to the wall and your hands behind your backs."

Dorange smiled at him.

"Surely you're not going to shoot us in the back, Mauron!"

"I shall choose how I shoot you. Do as I say."

They obeyed him. They both looked a bit self-conscious, like apprentice actors in a melodrama.

"This is it," thought Littlejohn to himself, and turned his head and smiled at Dorange, who smiled back at him like an old comrade now at the end of the road.

But nothing happened. Instead, there was a gasp and a thud, the men turned, and found Mauron, bleeding from the shoulder, the gun at his feet. As they moved, he was scrambling to recover it, but they reached him first. There was a scrimmage, which started so unexpectedly that it ended in nothing but disorder, a wild tangle of three bodies. Mauron with a supreme effort tore himself loose, reached the door first, slammed it and turned the key.

Dorange picked up the gun and fired a volley at the lock. Then he dragged the door open. As the two of them hurried after Mauron, Littlejohn got a glimpse through the open window of Knell and the Archdeacon running across the lawn.

Knell! Where the hell had he come from? Littlejohn sighed with relief as he followed Dorange across the hall. Mauron was zigzagging up the magnificent marble staircase three steps at a time, and Dorange was trying to get him within view to give him another round from the gun he was now carrying. But half-way across the hall the pursuers encountered obstacles.

The servant, Adolphe, took it upon himself to appear, trundling his trolley with more drinks. He pushed his equipment right in the path of Dorange and Littlejohn and the flying bottles and goblets gave Mauron just time to reach the first room on the balcony of the first floor. The door crashed-to after him and the lock clicked. Dorange hurried to the terrace below the windows of the room where Mauron had gone, to make sure that he did not escape that way.

Littlejohn climbed the stairs with long strides and ran along the landing. His first thrust against the door showed him that it was more than one man could force. The wood was of thick walnut and held like a rock.

Knell and the Archdeacon entered by the front door. The Inspector, still holding his rifle at the ready, looked surprised to see Littlejohn hanging over the wrought-iron rails of the balcony, waving to him. The Rev. Caesar Kinrade, whom nothing ever flurried, appeared quite used to such a hullaballoo and seemed to know what was going to happen next.

"Hullo, Knell! Just go through the *salon* there, relieve Inspector Dorange, who's guarding the windows of the room above, and ask him to join me here with his gun."

No sooner said, than done.

Then, a brief silence as the men below changed places. Their footsteps echoed on the stone of the terrace. The Archdeacon followed Knell, perhaps to get out of the way of the manoeuvres in progress.

The servant in the striped waistcoat chose the moment to enter with a brush and bucket. He came in stiffly, for he was wet-through from the contents of his ice-pail. He began uneasily to gather together the broken glass on the marble floor and drop it in his bucket. He looked up at Littlejohn reproachfully. He knew who was in the locked bedroom with his master and, in a fuddled kind of way, seemed to think Littlejohn was disturbing the fun.

"Get out!"

Dorange, entering, looked as if he could kill the flunkey. The man made mute gestures and pointed to the mass of bottles and implements. There were cocktail cherries all over the floor.

Suddenly, and before Dorange could reach the stairhead, there were noises in the bedroom and a shot was fired. Feet running across the parquet of the floor. The two detectives thrust their shoulders against the door, but it still refused to move. Dorange shot at the lock, but the door was barred behind.

There was a heavy oak chair in the hall and Littlejohn ran down again and carried it up. It took him all his time.

In the room more noises, more shouts. Then screams. A perfect shindy, as though the pair inside were throwing the furniture about.

"Don't... Don't... No..."

Another shot. Then heavy ponderous steps, like those of a lame man.

The door gave way under the battering from the heavy chair.

Monique Dol was stretched on the bed with a bullet wound in the head. The blood was oozing from the hole in her temple across the white silk counterpane. The room was a shambles. Broken ornaments, furniture, one of the curtains torn down, as though Mauron had chased her everywhere and she had thrown at him whatever she could lay her hands on. There was a piece of torn curtain in her hand, as if she had clung to it and he had wrenched her away.

There was another shot from below. The two detectives ran to the open window. The villa was built on a hillside and the ground sloped acutely to the road below. Mauron had leapt from the balcony, past the terrace beneath it and landed on a grassy lawn surrounded by mimosa bushes, and with a fountain and a statue in the middle. The bushes had broken his fall and he had tried to limp to the road below, still holding his revolver. Knell had shot him down from the terrace. He fell with a bullet in his leg, the gun flew from his hand, and as he crawled to retrieve it, Knell shot again and a bullet crashed between the hand outstretched and the weapon. Mauron withdrew, and then grabbed again. This time a bullet struck him in the wrist. Dorange crossed the terrace in long bounds, vaulted the balustrade, leapt across the lawn, and seized the now writhing Mauron by the scruff of the neck. He clenched his teeth, cast venomous looks around him, but never spoke again until an ambulance came and bore him away.

Knell seemed to think an apology was called for.

"What else could I have done, sir? He'd have got away and perhaps killed somebody else."

"Fine shooting, old man. Thanks for everything."

"I won the Manx rifle-shooting cup last year."

Littlejohn suddenly remembered that Pellepuits was missing. They found him trussed up in a lavatory behind the front door, where, he said, the chauffeur had bound and thrust him. He was none the worse for it. The chauffeur, it seemed, was the man whom Knell had laid-out and disarmed. He must have recovered and beat it, for there was no sign of him.

Pellepuits was fighting-mad when they released him. He drew his revolver and looked wildly around for somebody to shoot and they had to hastily disarm him, as he might have shot Knell, whom he seemed to suspect.

Later, after they had tidied themselves and allowed the shattered servant in the striped waistcoat to supply them with a bottle of whisky and glasses—he was too terrified and shaking even to pour out drinks—Littlejohn asked Knell what he was doing in France.

"The Chief Constable said I'd better follow you, sir, to represent the Manx police and in case you might need assistance. I came on a *Caravelle* which left an hour and a half after your Viscount but was in almost as soon, as they said your 'plane had met bad weather. I didn't know where you were, but you'd told me the Archdeacon was staying with Inspector Dorange. The police at Nice airport gave me his home 'phone number and I rang up Mr. Kinrade. He got one of Monsieur Dorange's men to drive him down to Nice, and we met there..."

The Rev. Caesar Kinrade interrupted him.

"He's too modest. He's been splendid! I knew the way to this villa and we motored to the end of the drive. I thought we'd better walk the rest. You see there was an armed man on the bank above the main gates. He must have thought we were a pair of trippers. He began to abuse us and told us that this was private property and in obscene language ordered us to clear off. We retreated as gracefully as we could, for the man was holding a rifle. Obviously he was on guard, so we judged that somewhere you were at a disadvantage. We therefore arranged that I should enter again, pretend to misunderstand the man, walk in at the gate boldly, and lure him to a mimosa thicket on the slope just above the gate. Knell climbed up the back and hid himself behind the copse. When the man, now threatening to shoot if I persisted, arrived on my heels at the thicket, this man..."

He pointed an accusing finger at Knell.

"... This man laid him unconscious with a single blow with the side of his hand."

Knell was still apologetic.

"You remember, don't you, that I was in the commandos in the war?"

"From where we stood, we could see Mauron through the open window holding the pair of you at bay with a tommy-gun. He was actually lining you both up for what looked like a firing-squad execution. Knell just couldn't contain himself."

"Why, sir, it was you who got angry! 'Cut him down', you said. 'And don't you dare miss him, or else...' So, I fired."

"And a damn good job you did..."

The members of the Parquet and the *Procureur* arrived, with a *juge d'instruction* in another car behind.

Dorange briefly explained what had happened. The *Procureur* couldn't believe his ears.

"Surely not Mauron?" he said.

"As far as I can judge, *M. le Procureur*, Mauron killed Monique Dol first and intended committing suicide. Then, when it came actually to doing it, he got cold feet. He was the kind who could never get used to doing his own dirty work. So, he jumped through the window and tried to get away."

"But Mauron! It can't be true!"

"Have you any money in Mauron's Bank, *M. le Procureur*?"

"What has that to do with you?"

"If you have, I'd advise you to withdraw it at once, sir. As soon as this case breaks in the newspapers, there'll be a run on the bank and little cash for the customers, I'd think. The bank's bust already."

The *Procureur* didn't wait to hear the rest. He rushed off to the nearest telephone.

Mauron was eventually sentenced to life imprisonment. It was a protracted case, for it took the members of the bar and the jury quite a long time to convince themselves that the great Mauron was a scoundrel. Even the judge had his doubts. Until a full report on Mauron's banking and other enterprises was made. He'd been living on his depositors for years. A verdict was then quickly arrived at. It did not greatly affect the stock exchanges of the world, which had other international fish to fry at the time. In London, a credit squeeze and a rise in Bank Rate to 7 per cent made Mauron's downfall seem insignificant.

Mauron is very busy in gaol. His appeal is in hand. His cell is full of books of law and he is sure that before long his sentence will be quashed. Meanwhile, he reads the world's financial papers every day, helps the governor of the gaol with his speculations and investments, and works hard on the details of many new companies he intends to promote and many new banks he will open. A number of his former depositors, including the judge himself and some of the jury, have sworn to shoot him if his appeal is successful.

The film, *Women Who Wait*, was finished after all, without Hal Vale and Monique Dol. Monique, who had a big funeral, was replaced in the cast by Angèle Tancerel, an even more sumptuous and dishevelled blonde, whose acting was well spoken of by many critics and earned the film an XX certificate. Littlejohn took his wife to see it. The miles of film shot on the Island had been boiled down to a mere ten minutes showing; the rest was studio work, mainly in bedrooms. They couldn't hear the dialogue for the background music.

Three murders, a financial bust-up on an international scale, and several bank failures. It seemed a lot to pay even for what a critic said was "a landmark in the cinema, a film to be remembered."

ABOUT THE AUTHOR

George Bellairs is the pseudonym under which Harold Blundell (1902–1982) wrote police procedural thrillers in rural British settings. He was born in Lancashire, England, and worked as a bank manager in Manchester. After retiring, Bellairs moved to the Isle of Man, where several of his novels are set, to be with friends and family.

In 1941 Bellairs wrote his first mystery, *Littlejohn on Leave*, during spare moments at his air raid warden's post. The title introduced Thomas Littlejohn, the detective who appears in fifty-seven of his novels. Bellairs was also a regular contributor to the *Manchester Guardian* and worked as a freelance writer for newspapers both local and national.

THE INSPECTOR LITTLEJOHN MYSTERIES

FROM OPEN ROAD MEDIA

OPEN ROAD
INTEGRATED MEDIA

Find a full list of our authors and titles at www.openroadmedia.com

FOLLOW US
@OpenRoadMedia

EARLY BIRD BOOKS
FRESH DEALS, DELIVERED DAILY

Love to read?
Love great sales?

Get fantastic deals on bestselling ebooks delivered to your inbox every day!

Sign up today at
earlybirdbooks.com/book

www.ingramcontent.com/pod-product-compliance
Lightning Source LLC
Chambersburg PA
CBHW021459020625
27587CB00006B/283